PENGUIN ARCHIVE
Stan the Killer

Georges Simenon
1903–1989
A PENGUIN SINCE 1950

Georges Simenon
Stan the Killer

Translated by Ros Schwartz

PENGUIN ARCHIVE

PENGUIN BOOKS

UK | USA | Canada | Ireland | Australia
India | New Zealand | South Africa

Penguin Books is part of the Penguin Random House group of companies whose addresses can be found at global.penguinrandomhouse.com.

Penguin Random House UK,
One Embassy Gardens, 8 Viaduct Gardens, London SW11 7BW

penguin.co.uk

First published in French in *Les Nouvelles Enquêtes de Maigret* by Gallimard in 1944
Published in *The New Investigations of Inspector Maigret* by Penguin Classics 2022
This selection published in Penguin Classics 2025
001

Translation copyright © Ros Schwartz, 2022
Les Nouvelles Enquêtes de Maigret copyright © 1944 Georges Simenon Limited, all rights reserved.
The New Investigations of Inspector Maigret copyright © 2022, all rights reserved.

GEORGES SIMENON and ® **Simenon.tm**®, all rights reserved

MAIGRET ® Georges Simenon Limited, all rights reserved

original design by Maria Picassó Piquer

No part of this book may be used or reproduced in any manner for the purpose of training artificial intelligence technologies or systems. In accordance with Article 4(3) of the DSM Directive 2019/790, Penguin Random House expressly reserves this work from the text and data mining exception.

Set in 11.2/13.75pt Dante MT Std
Typeset by Jouve (UK), Milton Keynes
Printed and bound in Great Britain by Clays Ltd, Elcograf S.p.A.

The authorized representative in the EEA is Penguin Random House Ireland, Morrison Chambers, 32 Nassau Street, Dublin D02 YH68

A CIP catalogue record for this book is available from the British Library

ISBN: 978–0–241–75216–6

Penguin Random House is committed to a sustainable future for our business, our readers and our planet. This book is made from Forest Stewardship Council® certified paper.

Contents

Stan the Killer	1
The Inn of the Drowned	43
Madame Maigret's Suitor	84

Stan the Killer

1

His hands behind his back and pipe between his teeth, Maigret moved slowly, edging his bulky frame through the throng in Rue Saint-Antoine, which burst into life every morning, the sunshine streaming down from a clear sky on to the little barrows piled high with fruit and vegetables, with one stall blocking almost the entire width of the pavement.

At this hour, housewives were out in force, weighing up artichokes and tasting cherries, while escalopes and rib steaks alternated on butchers' scales.

'Asparagus! Best asparagus, five francs a large bunch!'

'Fresh whiting! Straight off the docks!'

Kitchen boys in white aprons, butchers in fine-checked linen, the whiff of cheese outside a dairy and further on the aroma of roasted coffee; the entire bustling trade of small food shops and the procession of suspicious housewives, the ringing of cash registers and the rumble of passing buses . . .

No one suspected that it was Detective Chief Inspector Maigret who was making his way thus, or that he was working on one of the most disturbing cases imaginable.

Almost opposite Rue de Birague there was a small café, Le Tonnelet Bourguignon, whose narrow terrace had room for only three tables. Maigret seated himself there, with the air of a tired passer-by. He didn't even look up at the tall, thin waiter who came over to him and stood ready.

'A glass of white Mâcon,' grunted Maigret.

And who would have guessed that the waiter at Le Tonnelet Bourguignon, sometimes awkward in his movements, was none other than Inspector Janvier?

He returned with the glass of wine wobbling on a tray. He wiped the table with a dubious napkin and a slip of paper fluttered to the ground, which Maigret quickly picked up.

> The woman's out shopping. Haven't seen the Pirate. Bristles left early. The other three must still be at the hotel.

The crowd, at ten o'clock in the morning, was getting worse. Next to Le Tonnelet, a grocery shop was holding a sale and the barkers were stopping the passers-by to give them a sample of biscuits at two francs for a large tin.

On the corner of Rue de Birague, you could see the sign of a seedy hotel, one of those hotels with rooms 'by the month, the week or the day', not without 'payment in advance', and ironically this hotel was called Beauséjour.

Maigret savoured his dry white wine, and his gaze did not seem to be seeking out anything in particular

Stan the Killer

among the colourful horde milling around in the spring sunshine. And yet that gaze soon lighted on a first-floor window of a house in Rue de Birague, almost facing the hotel. At this window, a little old man was sitting beside a canary's cage seemingly with no other concern than to warm himself in the sun for as long as God deigned to grant him life.

It was Lucas, Sergeant Lucas, who had skilfully aged himself by twenty years or so and, although he had spotted Maigret on his terrace, was careful not to give him the slightest sign of recognition.

All this made up what is known in police-speak as a stakeout. It had been going on for six days, and Maigret came for an update at least twice a day, whereas at night his men were relieved by a local police officer who turned out to be an inspector from the Police Judiciaire, and by a streetwalker working the neighbourhood who avoided being accosted by punters.

Maigret would be given an update from Lucas later, when he received a phone call at Le Tonnelet Bourguignon. And most likely it would be no more earthshattering than Janvier's.

The crowd passed so close to the tiny terrace that Maigret kept having to tuck his feet in under his chair.

Then, suddenly, he was caught off guard when a man sat down next to him, at his own table, a thin, red-haired man with sad eyes, whose glum face had something clown-like about it.

'You again?' grunted Maigret.

3

'I apologize, Monsieur Maigret, but I am certain that in the end you will understand me and accept what I am suggesting.'

And, to Janvier who was coming over with the air of a perfect waiter:

'The same as my friend.'

He had a very strong Polish accent. He must have had a delicate throat, because he continuously chewed on a liquorice cigar which further emphasized his comic appearance.

'You're beginning to get on my nerves!' said Maigret ungraciously. 'Will you tell me how you knew that I would be here this morning?'

'I didn't know.'

'So, why have you come? Are you going to have me believe that you happened to run into me by chance?'

'No!'

The man's reflexes were slow, like those of the music-hall act known as the *acrobates flegmatiques*. He stared straight ahead with his jaundiced eyes, or rather he seemed to be staring vacantly. And he spoke in a flat, sad voice, as if he were reciting interminable condolences.

'You're mean to me, Monsieur Maigret.'

'You are not answering my question. How come you are here this morning?'

'I followed you!'

'From the Police Judiciaire?'

'Well before. From your home.'

'So, you admit that you are spying on me?'

'I am not spying on you, Monsieur Maigret. I have too

much respect and admiration for you! I have already told you that I'll be your colleague one day.'

And he sighed longingly as he contemplated his liquorice cigar with its fake glowing tip of painted wood.

The newspapers hadn't mentioned it, except one, and that newspaper – goodness knows how it had got wind of the case – was complicating Maigret's job even more.

> The police apparently have every reason to believe that a Polish crime gang, including Stan the Killer, are in Paris at present.

That was true, but it would have been better to hush it up. In four years, a group of Poles, about whom almost nothing was known, had attacked five farms, all in northern France, and always using the same methods.

First, these were all remote farmsteads belonging to old men. Furthermore, the attack invariably took place on the night of a fair, and on farms where, having sold a large number of animals, the owners had a large sum of cash in the house.

Nothing scientific in the method. A violent attack, as in the days of the highwaymen. Total disregard for human life.

The Poles murdered! They killed anyone who was in the farmhouse, even if there were children present, knowing that it was the only way to avoid being identified later on.

Were there two, five or eight of them?

In each case, people had noticed a van. A twelve-year-old kid claimed to have seen a one-eyed man.

Some stated that the robbers wore black masks.

The fact remains that on each occasion the farmers were stabbed with knives or, to be precise, had their throats slit.

The case was not under the jurisdiction of Paris. France's local Flying Squads were handling it.

For two years, the mystery had remained unsolved, which was of no consolation to rural communities.

Then, intelligence had come in from the Lille area, where there are villages that are real Polish enclaves. This intelligence was hazy. It was not even possible to identify the true source.

'The Poles claim that it's Stan the Killer's gang.'

But when the men in the miners' cottages were interviewed one by one – and most of them did not speak French – they knew nothing, or they'd stutter:

'I was told . . .'

'By whom?'

'I don't know . . . I've forgotten . . .'

When a murder was committed in the Reims area, however, a farm servant, whose existence must have escaped the robbers and who was asleep in an attic room, had been spared. She had heard the killers speaking in a language which she believed was Polish. She had merely glimpsed their faces covered by black masks, but she had noticed that one of the men had only one eye, and that another, a giant nearly six foot tall, was exceptionally hairy.

That was how in police circles they had come to refer to them as:

'Stan the Killer . . . Bristles . . . the Pirate . . .'

For months on end, they had learned nothing more,

until one day when a junior inspector from the Hotel Agency had made a discovery. He was in charge of the Saint-Antoine neighbourhood, which was teeming with Poles. He'd noticed, in a hotel in Rue de Birague, a dubious group which included a one-eyed man and a giant whose beard literally covered his face.

Outwardly, they appeared to be poor wretches. The hairy giant rented a room by the week, with his wife, but almost every night he gave shelter to several fellow Poles, sometimes two, sometimes five; often too, more Poles rented the adjacent room.

'Do you want to handle this, Maigret?' asked the chief superintendent of the Police Judiciaire.

But the next day, even though the case was hush-hush, a newspaper published the story!

The day after that, in his mail, Maigret found a clumsily scrawled letter, in an almost childish handwriting and with numerous spelling mistakes, on cheap paper of the sort sold in grocery shops:

> Stan won't let himself to be caught. Beware. Before you can get him, he'll have killed many people around him.

Admittedly, they didn't yet know the identity of Stan the Killer, but they had good reason to believe that the Rue de Birague lead was promising, since the killer was taking the trouble to write threatening letters.

And that letter was no joke, Maigret was convinced. It 'smelled of the truth', as he would say. And it left a sort of unsavoury aftertaste.

'Be careful, Maigret!' the chief had warned. 'No hasty arrests. The man who slit the throats of sixteen people in four years won't hesitate to empty his gun on those around him when he sees he's about to be caught.'

That was why Janvier had become a waiter opposite the Hôtel Beauséjour, while Lucas had transformed himself into a helpless old man who spent his days by his window soaking up the sun.

The neighbourhood carried on with its noisy life, oblivious to the fact that, from one moment to the next, a desperate man might fire at random around him.

'Monsieur Maigret, I've come to tell you . . .' And Michel Ozep had appeared.

His first encounter with Maigret had been four days earlier. He had turned up at the Police Judiciaire and insisted on seeing Maigret in person. Maigret had kept him waiting for two hours but that had not discouraged the fellow.

Once in the office, he had clicked his heels and bowed, proffering his hand:

'Michel Ozep, former Polish officer, gymnastics teacher in Paris.'

'Have a seat. What can I do for you?'

The Pole spoke with a pronounced accent and was so talkative that Maigret couldn't always follow him. He explained that he came from a very good family, that he had left Poland as a result of personal problems – he intimated that he was in love with his colonel's wife! – and that he was more despairing than ever because he couldn't get used to a mediocre existence.

Stan the Killer

'You see, Monsieur Maigret' (which he pronounced 'Maigrette') 'I am a gentleman. Here, I give lessons to people who have no culture and no education. I am poor.

'I decided to kill myself.'

Maigret's first thought was: 'A madman!'

Because Quai des Orfèvres was accustomed to visits of this kind as a good number of lunatics felt the need to come there to unburden themselves.

'I tried, three weeks ago. I threw myself into the Seine from the Pont d'Austerlitz, but the river police spotted me and pulled me out of the water.'

Making an excuse, Maigret went into the office next door, telephoned the river brigade and verified that it was true.

'Six days later, I wanted to gas myself in my apartment, but the postman came with a letter and opened the door.'

Phone call to the local police station. That too was true!

'I'm serious about wanting to kill myself, do you understand? My life is no longer worth living. A gentleman can't live in poverty like this or in mediocrity. So, I thought that perhaps you needed a man like me.'

'What for?'

'To help you arrest Stan the Killer.'

Maigret frowned.

'Do you know him?'

'No. I've simply heard about him. As a Pole, I am outraged that a fellow countryman of mine is thus violating the laws of hospitality. I want Stan and his gang to be arrested. I know that he has sworn to defend himself brutally. So, some of those who try to capture him are bound to get killed. Would it not be better if it were me, since I want to die anyway? Tell me where to find Stan. I'll go and disarm him. If need be, I'll wound him, so that he's no longer dangerous.'

Maigret was only able to give the standard response: 'Leave me your address. I'll write to you.'

Michel Ozep lived in furnished lodgings in Rue des Tournelles, not far from Rue de Birague, as it happened. An inspector had dealt with him. The report was rather in his favour. He had indeed been a sub-lieutenant in the Polish army when it was established. Then all trace of him disappeared. He surfaced in Paris, where he tried to give gymnastics lessons to the sons and daughters of small shopkeepers.

His suicide attempts were not invented.

Even so, Maigret, with the agreement of the head of the Police Judiciaire, had sent him an official letter ending:

> . . . to my great regret I cannot take advantage of your generous offer, for which I thank you . . .

Twice since then, Ozep had turned up at Quai des Orfèvres and insisted on seeing Maigret. The second time, he had even refused to leave, claiming that he would wait as long as necessary and occupying almost forcefully, for hours on end, one of the green-velvet chairs in the waiting room.

Now Ozep was there, at Maigret's table, on the terrace of Le Tonnelet Bourguignon.

Stan the Killer

'I want to prove to you, Monsieur Maigrette, that I am good for something and that you can accept my services. I have been following you for three days already and I can tell you everything you have done during that time. I also know that the waiter who has just served me is one of your men and that there's another one at a window across the street, beside a canary cage.'

Maigret furiously clenched his pipe stem between his teeth, not looking at Ozep, who was still talking in a toneless voice:

'I understand that when a stranger comes and tells you: "I am a former officer of the Polish army and I want to kill myself . . ." I understand that you thought: "Perhaps it's not true," but you checked up on everything I told you. You have seen that I don't stoop to lying.'

He talked incessantly, his words rapid, stilted, exhausting to listen to, especially since his accent distorted the syllables to the point where Maigret had to concentrate hard to follow.

'You are not Polish, Monsieur Maigrette. You don't understand the mentality. You don't speak the language. I am serious about helping you, I really am, because my country's reputation must not be tainted again by . . .'

Maigret was beginning to choke with rage. And Ozep, who must have been aware of it, still went on:

'If you try to capture Stan, what will he do? He might have two, maybe three guns in his pockets. He'll shoot everyone. Who knows whether little children might be killed, women injured? Then, people will say that the police . . .'

'Will you be quiet!'

'As for me, I am determined to die. No one will mourn poor Ozep. You tell me: "There's Stan!" and I follow him the way I've followed you. I wait until there's no one around. I say to him: "You are Stan the Killer!"'

'Then he shoots me, and I shoot him in the legs. Because he shoots me, you have the proof that he is indeed Stan and that you are not making a mistake. And, since he's wounded . . .'

He was unstoppable! He would have continued his spiel in defiance of the entire world.

'What if I had you locked up?' Maigret harshly interrupted.

'Why?'

'To get some peace!'

'What would you say? What has poor Ozep done to break the French laws which on the contrary he's prepared to defend and give his life for?'

'Shut up!'

'So? You agree?'

'Not at all!'

Just then, a woman walked past, a woman with fair hair and a very pale complexion, whom everyone in the neighbourhood was able to identify as a foreigner. She was carrying a shopping bag and heading towards a butcher's stall.

Maigret, who was gazing after her, noticed that his companion had a sudden urge to blow his nose loudly, while burying almost his entire face in his handkerchief.

'That's Stan's mistress, isn't it?' he said once the woman was out of sight.

'Are you going to leave me in peace, damn you?'

'You're convinced that she's Stan's mistress, but you don't know which one is Stan! You think he's the one with the beard. But the hairy one's called Boris . . . and the one-eyed guy is Sasha. He's Russian, not Polish. If you continue the investigation on your own, you won't find out anything because the hotel is full of Poles who'll refuse to answer you or will lie to you. Whereas I . . .'

None of the housewives in the teeming Rue Saint-Antoine had any idea of the matters being discussed on the tiny terrace of Le Tonnelet Bourguignon. The pale, blonde woman was bargaining over chops at a nearby butcher's stall and had the same weary expression in her eyes as Michel Ozep.

'Perhaps you're concerned because you're afraid that if I'm killed, you'll be asked for an explanation? First, I have no family. Second, I've written a letter in which I say that it is I who, alone and of my own free will, wanted to die.'

Poor Janvier, standing in the doorway, didn't know how to inform Maigret that there was a telephone message for him. Maigret had seen him but, puffing away on his pipe, he continued to keep an eye on his Pole.

'Listen, Ozep . . .'

'Yes, Monsieur Maigrette.'

'If you're seen again in the vicinity of Rue Saint-Antoine, I'll have you locked up!'

'But I live—'

'You'll just have to live somewhere else!'

'Are you refusing the offer I—'

'Off with you!'

'But—'

'Off with you, or I'll arrest you!'

The man rose, saluted with a click of his heels and gave a deep bow, then walked off with a dignified step. Maigret, who had noticed one of his men, had already signalled to him to follow the strange gymnastics teacher.

At last, Janvier could come over to him.

'Lucas has just called. He spotted guns in the room and five Poles slept in the adjoining room last night, some of them on the floor, leaving the communicating door halfopen. Who's that fellow?'

'No one. How much do I owe you?'

And Janvier, resuming his part, indicated Ozep's glass:

'Are you paying for the gentleman's drink? One franc twenty and one franc twenty, two forty.'

Maigret took a taxi to the Police Judiciaire

At the door to his office, he found the inspector he'd tasked with tailing Ozep.

'Did you lose him?' he thundered. Aren't you ashamed? It should have been child's play to shadow that man and—'

'I didn't lose him,' humbly muttered the inspector, who was a new boy.

'Where is he?'

'Here.'

'Did you bring him in?'

Stan the Killer

'It was him.'

Because Ozep had made a beeline for the Police Judiciaire and was sitting quietly in the waiting room eating a sandwich, having announced that he had an appointment with Detective Chief Inspector 'Maigrette'.

2

A less prestigious task, but useful nonetheless: Maigret, in his large handwriting, seeming to want to crush the nib against the paper, was writing a report summarizing the intelligence gathered from the various stakeouts over the past two weeks watching the Polish gang.

By bringing all the fragments together, he could see how scant the information they had was, since it wasn't even possible to establish how many individuals belonged to the gang.

According to previous intelligence, in other words statements from people who had glimpsed – or thought they had glimpsed – the robbers during the attacks, sometimes there were four, sometimes five of them, but it was likely that other accomplices identified the farms beforehand and visited the markets.

That amounted to six or seven people, which did seem to be the number of individuals hanging around the core group in Rue de Birague.

There were only three regular tenants, and they had filled in their forms and shown valid passports:

1. Boris Saft, the one the investigators had nicknamed Bristles and who seemed to be living as man and wife with the pale blonde woman;
2. Olga Tzerewski, age twenty-eight, born in Vilna;
3. Sacha Vorontzow, nicknamed the Pirate.

This trio was the focus of the investigation because they seemed to be the gang's ringleaders.

Boris 'Bristles' and Olga occupied one room.

Sacha the Pirate occupied the adjacent room and the communicating door between them was always open.

Each morning, the young woman went shopping and cooked meals on a spirit stove.

Bristles hardly ever went out, spending most of his days sprawled on the iron bed reading Polish newspapers, which he sent someone to buy for him from a newsstand on Place de la Bastille.

The Pirate had gone out on a few occasions, and each time he had been followed by a police officer. Was the man aware of it? Whether he was or not, he had merely wandered around Paris and stopped off at a few cafés for a drink, without saying a word to anyone.

The others were what Lucas called fly-by-nights. People came and went, always the same four or five. Olga fed them and sometimes they slept on the floor in one of the two rooms, then they left the following morning.

There was nothing unusual about this, because that was how it was almost throughout the hotel, which was home to poor people, exiles who banded together to pay for a room or who put up fellow countrymen they'd met in the street.

Maigret had a few notes on the fly-by-nights:

1. The Chemist, so called because he had twice presented himself at the labour exchange to apply for a job in a chemicals factory. His clothes were very shabby, but well tailored. He roamed the streets of Paris for hours on end with the air of someone seeking to earn a little money and, for one entire day, he had been taken on as a sandwichboard man;
2. Spinach, so called because he wore an incredible spinach-green hat which was all the more noticeable because his shirt was a faded pink. Spinach went out at night and he could be seen opening car doors outside some club in Montmartre;
3. Puffer, a short, fat wheezy man, better dressed than the others, even though he wore two odd shoes.

Two others came to Rue de Birague, less regularly, and it was hard to say whether they belonged to the gang. Maigret noted below this list:

> These people appear to be penniless foreigners seeking work of some kind. But there's always vodka in the rooms and some nights they have a real blow-out.
>
> It is impossible to know whether the gang is aware they are under surveillance and is behaving like this to confound the police.

On the other hand, if it is true that one of these individuals is Stan the Killer, most likely it is the Pirate or Bristles. But that is only a supposition.

He went to deliver his report to the chief without the slightest enthusiasm.

'No news?'

'Nothing specific. I could swear that the fellows have identified every one of our men and that they're mocking us by innocently coming and going all the time. They're telling themselves that we can't mobilize a section of the Police Judiciaire to watch them for ever. They are in no hurry.'

'Do you have a plan?'

'You know very well, chief, that thinking and I parted company a long time ago. I go, I come, I sniff. Some people believe I'm waiting for inspiration, but they're barking up the wrong tree. What I'm waiting for is the significant event that never fails to occur. The main thing is to be there when it does and to take advantage of it.'

'So, you're waiting for a little development?' muttered the chief, with a smile, because he knew his man.

'I'm convinced that we are dealing with the Polish gang. Because of that idiotic journalist, who is still prowling around the corridors and must have overheard a conversation, our pals know we're on to them.

'Now, why did Stan write? That's what I'm wondering. Maybe because he knows that the police are always reluctant to proceed with an arrest using force? Maybe, and this is the most likely, out of bravado. Killers have their pride – I was going to say professional pride.

'Which one is Stan?

'Why that nickname, which is more American than Polish?

'You know that I take my time to form an opinion. Well, it's beginning to take shape. Over the past couple of days, I've been getting the feeling that the psychology of my pals is very different from that of French killers.

'They need money, not to retire to the country or to live it up in nightclubs, or to run off overseas, but simply to live as they please, in other words enjoy an idle life, eating, drinking and sleeping, spending their days lying on a bed, no matter how filthy, smoking cigarettes and swigging bottles of vodka . . .

'They also want to be together, dream together, chat together and, some nights, sing together.

'In my view, after their first murder, they lived like this until they ran out of money, then they planned another attack. As soon as their funds get low, they begin again, coldly, without remorse, without the slightest pity for the old men whose throats they slit and whose savings they eat up in a few weeks or a few months . . .

'Now that I've understood that, I'm waiting . . .'

'I know! The little development . . .' teased the head of the Police Judiciaire.

'You can be as sarcastic as you like! The fact is that the little development has perhaps already happened.'

'Where?'

'In the waiting room. The fellow who calls me Maigrette and who is hell-bent on assisting me with the arrest, even if it costs him his life. He claims it is as good a way as any to commit suicide.'

'A nutcase?'

'Perhaps! Or an accomplice of Stan's who has found this means of learning of our intentions. Any supposition is valid and that is what makes my fellow so intriguing. What's to say, for example, that he isn't Stan in person?'

And Maigret emptied his pipe by banging it gently on the window-sill, the ashes falling on to the quay, perhaps onto the hat of a passer-by.

'Are you going to use this man?'

'I think so.'

With that, the chief superintendent reached the door, avoiding saying anything more.

'You'll see! I'd be surprised if the stakeout were still necessary after the end of this week.'

And it was already Thursday afternoon!

'Sit down there! Don't you get tired of sucking on that disgusting tar-flavoured liquorice cigar?'

'No, Monsieur Maigrette.'

'You really are getting very annoying with your Maigrette . . . But anyhow! Let's be serious. Are you still determined to die?'

'Yes, Monsieur Maigrette.'

'And do you still want to be given a dangerous mission?'

'I want to help you arrest Stan the Killer.'

Stan the Killer

'So, if I told you to go to up to the Pirate and shoot him in the legs, you would do it?'

'Yes, Monsieur Maigrette. But you would have to give me a gun. I'm very poor and—'

'Supposing now I ask you to go and tell Bristles, or the Pirate, that you have reliable information that the police are going to come and arrest them . . .'

'I'll be glad to, Monsieur Maigrette. I'll wait for the Pirate to walk past, and I'll give him the message.'

Maigret's ponderous gaze rested on the thin Pole, who did not appear to be disconcerted or worried. Rarely had Maigret seen such a combination of self-assurance and composure in a man.

Michel Ozep spoke of killing himself or of approaching the Polish gang as if it were perfectly simple, perfectly natural. He was equally at home on the terrace of the café in Rue Saint-Antoine as in the offices of the Police Judiciaire.

'You don't know either of them?'

'No, Monsieur Maigrette.'

'Well, I'm going to give you a job to do. Too bad for you if there's a punch-up!'

This time, Maigret half lowered his eyelids to hide the tension in his gaze.

'Later, the two of us will go to Rue Saint-Antoine. I'll wait for you outside. You will choose a time when the woman is alone and go up to the room. You will tell her that you are a fellow Pole and that you happen to have learned that the police are planning to raid the hotel that night.'

Silence from Ozep.

'Do you understand?'

'Yes.'

'Are we agreed?'

'I want to tell you something, Monsieur Maigrette.'

'Are you chickening out?'

'I'm not doing what you say . . . "chickening out" . . . No! It's just that I'd like to do things differently Perhaps you think I'm very daring . . . is that the word? But with women, I'm very shy . . . and women are clever, much cleverer than men. So she'll be able to tell that I'm lying . . . and because I know that she'll see that I'm lying, I'll go red . . . and when I go red . . .'

Maigret didn't move, allowing him to tie himself in knots in an explanation that was as convoluted as it was feeble.

'I prefer to talk to a man. To the one with the beard, if you like, or the one you call the Pirate, or anyone.'

Perhaps because a shaft of sunlight fell into the room and shone directly on Maigret's face, he appeared to be snoozing, like a man who has eaten a copious lunch and needs to have a nap in his chair.

'It's exactly the same thing, Monsieur Maigrette . . .'

But Monsieur Maigrette didn't reply and the only sign of life he gave was a thin spiral of blue smoke rising from the bowl of his pipe.

'I'm sorry. You can ask me anything, but you are asking me to do the one thing . . .'

'Shut up!'

'Pardon?'

'I say "shut up"! In other words, just be quiet. Where did you meet the woman, Olga Tzerewski?'

'Me?'

'Answer!'

'I don't understand what you mean . . .'

'Answer!'

'I don't know that woman. If I knew her, I'd tell you. I am a former officer of the Polish army and if I hadn't had bad luck—'

'Where did you meet her?'

'I swear to you, Monsieur Maigrette, on the heads of my poor mother and my poor father . . .'

'Where did you meet her?'

'I wonder why you have turned so nasty towards me! You are speaking to me harshly! And I came here to offer you my services, to prevent French people from being killed by one of my fellow countrymen . . .'

'*Chante, fifi!*'

'Pardon?'

'*Chante, fifi!* That means in French: carry on with your claptrap but it won't wash with me.'

'Ask anyone . . .'

'That is what I am doing!'

'Ask me something else, to throw myself under a Metro train or jump out of the window . . .'

'I am asking you to go and see this woman and tell her that tonight we will be arresting the gang . . .'

'You absolutely insist?'

'You are free to say yes or no!'

'And if I say no?'

'You can go hang yourself!'

'Why hang?'

'It's an expression. I mean you would do well not to get in my way again.'

'Are you really arresting the gang tonight?'

'Probably!'

'And will you let me help you?'

'Possibly. We'll see about that when you have carried out your first mission.'

'At what time?'

'Your mission?'

'No! What time will the arrest be?'

'Let's say one o'clock in the morning.'

'I'm going.'

'Where?'

'To find the woman.'

'Wait! We'll leave together!'

'It's best if I go alone. If they see us, they'll realize that I'm helping the police.'

Of course, Ozep had barely left his office when Maigret put an inspector on his tail.

'Do I stay out of sight?' asked the inspector.

'Don't bother. He's smarter than you and he knows very well that I'm going to have him followed.'

And, without wasting a second, Maigret went downstairs and jumped into a taxi.

'As fast as you can, to the corner of Rue de Birague and Rue Saint-Antoine.'

It was a glorious afternoon and colourful awnings over the shops added a cheerful note. In the shade, dogs stretched out and life went by at a leisurely pace; it

Stan the Killer

seemed as if even the buses were struggling to rev up in the heavy atmosphere, their fat tyres leaving tracks on the hot tarmac.

Maigret leapt out of the taxi into the building that formed the corner of the two streets, and, on the second floor, he opened a door, without taking the trouble to knock, and found Lucas sitting at the window, still disguised as a quiet, nosey old man.

The room was shabby and not very clean. On the table sat the remains of a cold meal that Lucas had had delivered from a delicatessen.

'Any news, inspector?'

'Is there anyone opposite?'

The room had been chosen for its strategic position, as you could see straight into the two rooms of the Hôtel Beauséjour that were occupied by the Poles.

Because of the heat, all the windows were open, including that of another room where a scantily dressed young woman could be seen sleeping.

'Well, well! I see you've got plenty to look at . . .'

On a chair, a pair of binoculars showed that Lucas was doing his job conscientiously and was intent on noting every detail.

'At the moment,' he replied, 'there are two of them in the rooms, but soon there'll only be one person.'

And it was true, the man was getting dressed. He had stayed in bed all morning, as was his habit.

'Is that Bristles?'

'Yes. There were three of them at lunch: Bristles, the woman and the Pirate. Then the Pirate left almost immediately. Bristles got up and started to get washed and dressed. Look! He's just put on a clean shirt, which he doesn't do very often.'

Maigret had gone over to the window and was now taking a peek. The hairy giant was putting on a tie over his shirt, its whiteness contrasting sharply with the grey walls.

You could see his lips moving as he admired himself in the mirror. And, behind him, the blonde woman was tidying up, picking up greasy papers which she screwed up into a ball, and finally turning off a spirit stove.

'If only we knew what they were saying to each other!' sighed Lucas. 'There are times when I get really annoyed! I can see them talking, talking endlessly; sometimes they gesticulate, and I can't guess what it's about. I'm beginning to realize what hell it must be not to be able to hear, and I understand why deaf people are seen as unpleasant people . . .'

'That's enough talk for now! Do you think the woman is going to stay there?'

'It's not her usual time for going out. If she were to, she'd have put on her grey suit.'

Olga was in fact wearing the same little dark woollen dress that she'd worn that morning to do her shopping. As she went about clearing up the bohemian household, she smoked a cigarette without ever removing it from her mouth, as if she were one of those hardened smokers who need tobacco all day long.

Stan the Killer

'She barely ever speaks!' commented Maigret.

'It's not her usual time for that either. She mostly talks in the evening, when they're all gathered around her. Or on some occasions, when she's alone with the one I call Spinach, which is rare. Either I'm very much mistaken or she has a soft spot for Spinach, who's the most attractive of the bunch.'

It was a curious feeling to be in a strange room staring into the home of people whose routines and slightest actions had become familiar.

'You're turning into a real concierge, Lucas!'

'That's what I'm here for, isn't it? Listen, I can even tell you that the girl next door, the one who's fast asleep, made love last night until three o'clock in the morning with a young man who wore a cravat and left at dawn, probably to steal back to his parents' house. Aha! Bristles is on his way out.'

'I say! He looks almost smart.'

'That's one way of putting it . . . He appears more like a fairground wrestler than a man of the world.'

'Let's say a very successful fairground wrestler!' conceded Maigret.

Across the street, no prolonged goodbyes. The man simply left, in other words, disappeared from the area of the room that could be seen from the policeman's vantage point.

A little after that, he stepped into the street and headed in the direction of Place de la Bastille.

'Derain will tail him,' announced Lucas, who was like a big spider at the centre of his web. 'But Bristles knows he's being followed. He'll just walk around and maybe have a drink at a pavement café.'

Meanwhile, the woman took a road map out of a drawer and spread it out on the table. Maigret calculated that Ozep wouldn't have come by taxi but by Metro, and wouldn't get there for a few minutes yet.

'If he comes!' he corrected himself.

And he did come! They saw him arrive, hesitant, and then pace up and down the street, while the police inspector following him pretended to be interested in a fishmonger's in Rue Saint-Antoine.

Seen from above, the scrawny Pole looked even thinner, even more insignificant, and Maigret had a momentary twinge of conscience.

He thought he heard the poor fellow's voice repeating his famous 'Monsieur Maigrette' over and over again, amid his convoluted explanations.

He was undecided, that was certain. You could even have sworn he was frightened, and he kept glancing around with evident anxiety.

'Do you know what he's looking for?' asked Maigret.

'The pale guy? No! Maybe money to pay for the hotel?'

'He's looking for me. He's aware that I'm probably in the vicinity and hoping that by some miracle I've changed my mind.'

Too late! Michel Ozep had just headed into the hotel's dark passageway. They could follow him in their mind's eye. He climbed the stairs and reached the second floor.

'He's still dithering,' said Maigret.

Because the door should already have opened!

'He's on the landing . . . He's going to knock . . . He's knocked . . . Well, well!'

The young blonde woman gave a start, instinctively put her road map away in the wardrobe and went over to the door.

For a moment, they couldn't see anything. The two characters were standing in the part of the room that was hidden from view.

Then, all of a sudden, the woman appeared and there was something different about her. Her movements were sharp, rapid. She went straight over to the window, closed it and drew the dark curtains.

Lucas turned to Maigret and pulled a funny face.

'Well, well, well!'

But he stopped joking when he saw that Maigret was a lot more concerned than he'd anticipated.

'What time is it, Lucas?'

'Ten past three.'

'Do you think there's a chance that one of our shysters will come back shortly?'

'I don't think so. Other than Spinach, as I've told you, if he thinks that Bristles is out. You seem worried.'

'I don't like the way that window was closed.'

'Are you afraid for your Pole?'

Maigret said nothing, and Lucas went on:

'Has it occurred to you that there's no proof he's in the room? We saw him enter the hotel, true, but he could well have gone into another room . . . and it might be someone else who . . .'

Maigret shrugged and sighed:

'Enough! You're wearing me out.'

3

'What time is it, Lucas?'

'Twenty past three.'

'Do you know what's going to happen?'

'Do you want to go and see what's going on across the street?'

'Not yet. But I'm probably about to make a fool of myself. Where can we telephone from?'

'The next room. He's a garret tailor who works for a big fashion house that insists he has a telephone.'

'In that case, go to your tailor's. Try to ensure he doesn't overhear the conversation. Call the chief for me and tell him to send around twenty armed officers as a matter of urgency. They're to spread out around the Hôtel Béausejour and wait for my signal.'

Lucas' expression reflected the seriousness of this order, which was quite unusual for Maigret, who readily mocked police operations.

'Do you think things are going to turn nasty?'

'Unless they already have.'

He did not take his eyes off the window with grubby panes and the crimson velvet curtains that dated from the last century.

When Lucas returned, he found Maigret in the same spot, his brow still as furrowed.

'The chief says to be careful. Already last week an

inspector was killed, and if there were to be another accident . . .'

'Be quiet, will you?'

'Do you believe that Stan the Killer . . . ?'

'I don't believe anything! I've thought so much about this case since this morning that I've got a headache. For now, I'm following my hunches, and if you want to know everything, unfortunately, I have a hunch that something bad is happening, or is about to happen. What time?'

'Twenty-three.'

As if ironically, in the room next door, the girl was still asleep, her mouth half open, her legs drawn up. Higher up, on the fifth or sixth floor, someone was trying to play the accordion, beginning the same dance-hall tune over and over again, with wrong notes.

'Do you want me to go over there?' Lucas offered.

Maigret glared at him, as if his subordinate were chastising him for his lack of courage.

'What is that supposed to mean?'

'Nothing! I can see that you're worried by what's going on across the street, and I'm offering to go and see—'

'And do you think I'd hesitate to go there myself? You're forgetting one thing: once over there, it's too late. If we go there and find nothing, we'll never discover any more about the gang. That's why I'm hesitating. If only that minx hadn't shut the window!'

Suddenly, he frowned.

'Hold on! The other times, she never closed the window, did she?'

'Never!'

'So, she didn't suspect your presence here.'

'She probably took me for a senile old man.'

'And so, it didn't occur to her to shut the window, but the fellow who went in . . .'

'Ozep?'

'Him or another. The person who went in told the woman to close the window before showing himself.'

He picked up his hat from the chair where he'd left it, emptied his pipe and filled it, tamping down the tobacco with his forefinger.

'Where are you going, chief?'

'I'm waiting for our men to get here. Look! There are two of them down there by the bus stop . . . And in that stationary taxi, I recognize more of our people. If I stay inside for five minutes without opening the window, you come in with some men.'

'Have you got your gun?'

A few moments later, Maigret crossed the street, while Janvier, who had spotted him, stopped wiping the tables on his terrace.

Lucas, feverish, held his watch in his hand, but as often happens when a person is overzealous, he had forgotten to take note of the time Maigret went into the hotel, so he wasn't able to tell when the five minutes were up.

He didn't need to worry, however, because, after what seemed to him to be a miraculously short time, the window opposite opened. A Maigret more disgruntled than ever signalled to Lucas to come and join him.

Lucas' impression was that the room was empty apart

from Maigret, but when he entered, after stumbling up a gloomy staircase that smelled of stale food and toilets, he gave a start on seeing a woman's body lying at his feet.

A quick glance at Maigret, who replied:

'Dead, of course!'

It was as if the murderer had wanted to leave his signature, because the victim's throat had been slit, like all of Stan's victims. There was blood everywhere, on the bed and on the floor, and the killer had wiped his hands on the towel, which was bloodstained a reddish-brown.

'Was it him?'

Maigret, standing stock still in the middle of the room, gave a shrug.

'Shall I give his description to our men and tell them to ensure he doesn't leave the hotel?'

'If you like.'

'I'm inclined to put an officer on the roof, in case . . .'

'Fine.'

'Shall I inform the chief?'

'Later.'

It wasn't easy to talk to Maigret when he had that look on his face! Besides, Lucas put himself in the shoes of his chief, who had said himself that everyone was going to laugh at him.

Now, it would be worse than ridicule. He had mobilized a large number of police officers, but it had already been too late, whereas a murder was being committed under Maigret's very nose, almost with his approval, since he was the one who had sent Ozep to the Hôtel Beauséjour!

'If any of the gang come back, should I arrest them?'

A nod. Or rather a gesture of indifference. And Lucas finally left. Maigret remained alone in the middle of that room where the open window let in the bright sunlight.

He mopped his forehead and automatically relit his pipe, which he'd allowed to go out.

'What time is it?'

Then he remembered that he was alone and took his fob watch from his pocket. It was three thirty-five and the accordion upstairs was still squealing, but that didn't prevent the young woman next door from sleeping like an innocent animal.

'Where is Maigret?' asked the head of the Police Judiciaire, alighting from a car and finding himself faced with Lucas.

'In the room. It's number 19, on the second floor. The hotel staff don't know anything yet.'

A few moments later, the chief found Maigret sitting on a chair in the middle of the room, close to the body. Maigret was smoking, a grim expression on his face. He barely noticed the arrival of the big boss.

'Well, it looks as if we're in a fine mess, my friend!'

All he got out of Maigret was a noncommittal grunt.

'So, the notorious killer was none other than the fellow who came to offer you his services! Admit, Maigret, that you might have been suspicious, and that Ozep's behaviour was ambiguous to say the least . . .'

There was a deep vertical crease down Maigret's

Stan the Killer

forehead, and his jaw was thrust forward, making his entire appearance strikingly powerful.

'Do you think he's been unable to get out of the hotel?'

'I'm certain of it,' retorted Maigret, seeming not to attach any importance to the question.

'Haven't you searched for him?'

'Not yet.'

'Do you think he'll give himself up easily?'

Then Maigret's gaze slowly switched away from the window and towards the commissioner and rested heavily on him. There was a solemnity in this deliberateness, in this hesitation, in the ambiguity of his words.

'Unless I'm mistaken, the man will try to kill a number of people before allowing himself to be caught. Unless I'm mistaken, things will proceed of their own accord.'

'I don't understand, Maigret. Do you still doubt that Stan and your Ozep are one and the same person?'

'I am convinced that earlier, there were two people in this room, and that one of them was Stan the Killer.'

'So . . .'

'I repeat, chief: I can be wrong, just like anyone else. In that case, I apologize, because things will turn ugly. I'm not satisfied with the way this business seems to be unravelling. I sense that something's not right. If Ozep were Stan, there'd be no reason for—'

'Go on!'

'It would take too long. What time do you make it, chief?'

'Four fifteen. Why?'

'No reason . . .'

'Are you staying here, Maigret?'

'Until further orders, yes.'

'Meanwhile, I'll go down and see what our men are doing.'

They had arrested Spinach, who, as Lucas had predicted, had come to visit the young woman. The Pole had been informed that his fellow countrywoman had been killed and had turned ashen, but he hadn't batted an eyelid when Ozep's name had been mentioned.

'She can't be dead!' was all he said, several times over, as he was being taken to the police station.

When Maigret was told about this arrest, he merely grunted:

'Don't give a damn!'

And he resumed his strange communion with the dead woman. Half an hour later, it was the Pirate's turn to come back and be arrested as soon as he stepped over the threshold. He too let himself be apprehended without raising an eyebrow, but when he was told about the young woman's death, he tried to shake off his handcuffs and race upstairs.

'Who's done this?' he yelled. 'Who killed her? It's you lot, isn't it?'

'It's Ozep, otherwise known as Stan the Killer . . .'

The man quietened down as if by magic, and repeated with a frown:

'Ozep?'

'You're not going to have us believe that you don't know your boss?'

Stan the Killer

It was the chief in person who proceeded with this hasty questioning, in a corridor, and he had the impression that a faint smile flitted across the prisoner's lips.

One of the accomplices followed, the one they called the Chemist. He merely replied to all their questions looking perfectly horrified, as if he'd never heard of the young woman, or of Ozep, or Stan.

Maigret was still upstairs, mulling over the same problem, trying to find the key that would enable him at last to understand what was going on.

'That's enough!' he muttered when he was told about the arrest of Bristles, who, after doing his damnedest to resist, had begun to cry like a baby.

All of a sudden, Maigret looked up at Lucas, who had brought him the news.

'Haven't you noticed something?' he said. 'That's four of them who we've arrested one after the other, and not one of them put up a real fight, whereas a man like Stan . . .'

'But since Stan is Ozep . . .'

'Have you found him?'

'Not yet. We had to wait until all the accomplices were back before turning the hotel upside-down, otherwise they'd have smelled something from a long way off and wouldn't have fallen into the trap. Now we've got nearly all of them, the big boss has begun to lay siege to the place. The men are downstairs and are going to search the hotel with a fine-tooth comb, from the cellar to the attic if there is one.'

'Listen to me, Lucas . . .'

And Lucas, who was about to leave, stayed for a moment, feeling something akin to pity for Maigret.

'Yes, chief?'

'The Pirate isn't Stan. Spinach isn't Stan. Bristles isn't Stan. But I am convinced that Stan was living in this hotel and was the leader the others congregated around!'

Lucas preferred to say nothing, leaving Maigret to pursue his pet theory.

'If Ozep was Stan, he had no reason to come here and kill an accomplice. If he wasn't Stan . . .'

Abruptly, rising with such a rapid movement that Lucas jumped:

'Look at this woman's shoulder, just in case . . . The left, yes.'

He too leaned over. Lucas pulled aside her dress, revealing her very pale flesh, and on that flesh, the mark with which the Americans brand women criminals.

'Did you see, Lucas?'

'But chief . . .'

'Don't you see? She was Stan! I'd read something along those lines, but I didn't make the connection, so convinced was I that our Stan was a man. Four or five years ago, a young woman in America, the ringleader of a criminal gang, led attacks on isolated farmsteads, just like the ones here. Just as here, the victims had their throats slit, by the hand of this woman whose savagery the American papers revelled in describing.'

'Is it her?'

'It's almost certainly her . . . but I'll know in an hour,

Stan the Killer

if I can find the relevant documents. I'd cut out a few pages from a magazine. Are you coming, Lucas?'

Maigret dragged his subordinate down the stairs. On the ground floor, he ran into the big boss.

'Where are you going, Maigret?'

'To Quai des Orfèvres, chief. I think I've got it. In any case, I'm taking Lucas with me, and he'll come back and let you know.'

And Maigret tried to find a taxi, without noticing that people were giving him strange looks – a mixture of anger and pity.

'What about Ozep?' asked Lucas, clambering into the car.

'That is exactly what I'm going to investigate. I mean I hope to find some information about him. If he killed that woman, it was because he had his reasons. Listen, Lucas: when I wanted to send him to talk to the others, he agreed straight away. On the other hand, when I asked him to deliver a message to the woman, he refused and I had to demand, even threaten. In other words, the others didn't know him, but the woman did.'

As might have been expected, it took more than half an hour to lay hands on the file, because organization wasn't Maigret's forte, despite his placid air.

'Read! Bear in mind that the Americans like to exaggerate to give readers their money's worth. "The vampire woman" . . . "The Polish woman killer" . . . "A twenty-three-year-old gang boss".'

The articles jubilantly described the exploits of the Polish woman along with numerous photographs.

At eighteen, Stephanie Polintskaia was already known to the Warsaw police. At around this time, she met a man who made her his wife and tried to curb her evil instincts. She had a child by him, but one day, on coming home from work, the man found the baby with its throat slit. As for the woman, she had run off with all the money and the few valuables there were in the house.

'Do you know who that man was?' asked Maigret.

'Ozep?'

'Here's a photo of him that is a perfect likeness! Which proves that we ought to know the criminal archives of every country in the world by heart. Do you understand now? Stephanie, known as Stan to her family and friends, struck in America. How she avoided being sent to prison there, I have no idea. The fact remains that she fled to France where she continued her exploits, without changing anything of her method, having surrounded herself, as she did there, with a band of thugs.

'The husband learns from the newspapers that she is in Paris, that the police are on her trail. Does he want to save her again? I don't think so. I am rather inclined to think that he would like to be certain that the vile murderer of his child won't escape punishment. That's why he offered me his services.

'He doesn't have the courage to act alone. He's a weakling, a ditherer . . .

'He wants the police to act with his help, and it is I who, this afternoon, in a way pushed him to do the deed.

'Face to face with his ex-wife, what choice did he have? Kill or be killed, because, once she realized she had been

Stan the Killer

unmasked, she would certainly not have balked at getting rid of the only man capable of denouncing her.

'So, he killed! And shall I tell you something? I bet we'll find him in some corner of the hotel, possibly injured; after two failed suicide attempts, I wouldn't be surprised if he'd failed a third time. Now, you can go back there and tell the chief—'

'No need!' said the commissioner's voice. 'Stan the Killer hanged himself in a room on the sixth floor whose door he'd found open. Good riddance!'

'Poor fellow!' sighed Maigret.

'You're sorry for him.'

'Oh yes, I am. Especially as I am partially to blame for his death. I don't know if I'm getting old, but it took me a long time to find the solution.'

'What solution?' asked the head of the Police Judiciaire with a suspicious look.

'The solution to the entire problem!' said Lucas, delighted to put in a word. 'Maigret has just pieced together the entire story in detail and, when you came in, he was saying that we'd find Ozep in some corner where he would have tried to kill himself.'

'Is that true, Maigret?'

'It is true. You know, as a result of pondering the same question . . . I don't think I have ever been so angry in all my life. I could sense that the solution was there, within reach, that it would take only a tiny thing. You were all buzzing around me like big fat flies and talking to me about accomplices who didn't interest me. Well, there we are!'

He took a deep breath, filled his pipe and asked Lucas for matches because he had used up all of his own during the afternoon.

'I say, chief! It's seven o'clock. How about the three of us going for a nice cool beer? On condition that Lucas removes his wig and makes himself presentable.'

And they were sitting in the Brasserie Dauphine, when suddenly Maigret smacked his forehead. He had just glanced automatically at the waiter.

'What about Janvier?' he asked.

'What?'

'Has he not been relieved of his duty? Poor thing! When I think that while we're sitting here drinking beers, he's still doomed to serve them!'

The Inn of the Drowned

I

'Are you sure you don't want to shelter from the rain?' insisted the captain of the gendarmerie, somewhat awkwardly.

And Maigret, his hands in his overcoat pockets, his bowler hat acting as a water trap that emptied itself at the slightest movement, the sullen, burly, motionless Maigret on a bad day, his pipe firmly clenched between his teeth, growled:

'No!'

One thing that has to be said is that the irritating cases, the ones you have all the difficulties in the world to extricate yourself from and which always end up badly, are always the ones you get drawn into stupidly, by chance, or simply for lack of the energy to say no while there's still time.

This applied to Maigret, once again. He had come to Nemours the previous day for a minor case which he needed to discuss with Captain Pillement.

The captain was a charming man, cultured and athletic, who came from Saumur. He had insisted on regaling Maigret with the delights of his table and his wine cellar, and, since the rain was bucketing down, he had invited him to stay in his guest room.

Autumn was at its grimmest and for two weeks the weather had been wet and foggy, while branches were swept along by the muddy waters of the Loing in spate.

'This was bound to happen!' sighed Maigret when, at six o'clock in the morning, before it was even daylight, he heard the telephone ringing.

A few moments later, the captain was mumbling outside his door:

'Are you asleep, inspector?'

'No, I'm not asleep!'

'Do you mind coming with me? There's been a curious accident fifteen kilometres from here.'

Maigret had gone, of course! To the banks of the Loing, between Nemours and Montargis, where the main road runs parallel to the river. A landscape that would put you off getting out of bed early in the morning. A low, cold sky. Slanting sheets of rain. The river a dirty brown and, beyond, poplar trees bordering the canal.

Not a single village. The only inn, the Fishermen's Inn, was seven hundred metres away, and Maigret already knew that the locals called it the Inn of the Drowned.

As for the drowned on this occasion, nothing was known about them yet! The crane squeaked while two men in oilskins, like sailors, could be seen operating the pump of an aqualung. Some half-dozen cars had stopped by the roadside. Others travelling in both directions

The Inn of the Drowned

slowed down, sometimes pulling up to find out what was going on and then continuing on their way.

There were uniformed gendarmes and ambulances that had been called out on standby during the night but were clearly no longer of any use.

They had to wait, wait until the car that was midstream, under the fast-flowing waters, was firmly attached to the crane and hoisted out of the river.

A ten-tonne lorry, one of those foul-smelling monsters that travel up and down the major roads, was parked before the bend.

No one was sure exactly what had happened. The previous evening, the ten-tonne lorry, which made a regular trip between Paris and Lyon, was driving along this same road, shortly after eight p.m. On the bend, it had hit a car that was stationary, with all its lights off, and the car had been flung into the Loing.

The driver, Joseph Lecoin, thought he'd heard shouts, and the bargeman from *La Belle Thérèse*, which was moored in the canal less than one hundred metres away, claimed that he too heard cries for help.

The two men had met on the bank and had searched as best they could with a lantern. Then the lorry driver had carried on to Montargis where he'd reported the accident to the gendarmerie.

The spot where the accident had taken place was under the jurisdiction of Nemours, and the local gendarmerie had also been informed, but, since they could do nothing until daylight, it was only at six a.m. that the lieutenant had roused his captain.

It was dismal. They were all cold and stood with hunched shoulders, darting barely anxious glances at the muddy waters.

The owner of the inn was there, sheltering under a huge umbrella, and he discussed the matter like an expert.

'Unless the bodies are trapped in the car, they won't be recovered for ages, because all the dams are broken and they'll reach the Seine, if they don't get caught up in some roots.'

'They are very unlikely to be in the car still,' replied the lorry driver, 'because it's an open-topped car!'

'That's strange!'

'Why?'

'Because yesterday I had two young customers in an open-topped car. They stayed and dined at the inn. They were planning to also stay last night, but I didn't see them again.'

It cannot be said that Maigret was listening to this chatter, but he couldn't help hearing and taking note.

The underwater diver finally surfaced, and people hurried to unscrew his heavy metal helmet.

'Go ahead,' he said. 'The hoist is firmly attached.'

On the road, cars were hooting, unaware of the cause of this gathering. Heads appeared out of the doors.

The crane, which had been brought from Montargis, made a horrendous racket and at last the top of a grey car emerged from the water, then the bonnet and the wheels.

Maigret's feet were wet, and his trouser legs were

The Inn of the Drowned

muddy. He'd have loved a cup of hot coffee, but he didn't want to leave the scene to go to the inn, and the captain of the gendarmerie didn't dare try to distract him. 'Careful boys! . . . A bit more room on the left . . .'

The front of the car showed clear evidence of the collision, proving that, at the time of the accident, as the lorry driver had said, the roadster had been facing towards Paris.

'Heave! . . . One . . . Two . . . Heave!'

Finally, the car was on the riverbank. A strange contraption, with buckled wheels, its wings crumpled like paper, the seats already covered in mud and debris.

The lieutenant made a note of the registration number, while the captain looked on the dashboard for the owner's nameplate. This plate bore the name: *R. Daubois, 135, Avenue des Ternes, Paris.*

'Shall I have someone phone there, inspector?'

Maigret appeared to indicate: 'Do as you like! It's none of my business!'

That was a job for the gendarme and not an inspector from the Police Judiciaire. A sergeant had already ridden off on a motorbike to telephone Paris. Everyone, including a dozen onlookers who had got out of their cars, stood around the wreck salvaged from the water, and some were feeling the bodywork or leaning in to see the interior.

It was one of the onlookers who had the curiosity to try the handle of the boot. Unexpectedly, given how mangled the vehicle was, the door opened easily, and the man gave a shout and took two or three steps backwards while some rushed over to see.

Maigret drew near too. He frowned and, for the first time that morning, made his voice heard other than in a grunt:

'Back everyone! Do not touch anything!'

He had seen it too. A human form, strangely contorted, squashed into the boot of the convertible as if someone had struggled to shut the body in it. On top of the heap, platinum blonde hair revealed that this was a woman.

'Captain! Clear the area, would you? There's a development, a rather ugly one.'

And an ugly task ahead! Simply extricating the woman's body from the luggage well dripping with water was bad enough!

'Can you smell that?'

'Yes.'

'You don't think that . . .'

Oh yes! They had the proof a quarter of an hour later. One of the bystanders was a doctor. He examined the body on the grass verge. They had to keep moving back the people and even the children who wanted to see.

'She's been dead for at least three days.'

Someone was tugging at Maigret's sleeve. It was Justin Rozier, the owner of the Inn of the Drowned.

'I recognize the car,' he stated, taking pleasure in keeping everyone guessing. 'It belongs to my customers!'

'Do you have their names?'

'They filled in their form.'

The doctor broke in:

'You realize this is a murder?'

The Inn of the Drowned

'Committed with what?'

'A razor. The woman's throat has been slit.'

And it was still raining, on the car and on the body and on all those dark shapes milling around in the gloom.

A motorbike. The sergeant leapt off.

'The car doesn't belong to Monsieur Daubois any more. I spoke to him in person on the telephone. He sold it last week to a garage-owner at Porte Maillot.'

'What about the garage-owner?'

'I telephoned. The garage sold the car three days ago to a young man who paid cash, so they didn't take his name.'

'But I've got his name!' protested the innkeeper who felt no one was paying him enough attention. 'Just come to my place and . . .'

First, they witnessed the arrival of a redhead who was the editor of the only Montargis newspaper and the correspondent for a major Paris daily. Goodness knows how he conducted his inquiries because Maigret sent him packing, as did Captain Pillement, which didn't stop him from monopolizing the telephone booth for more than fifteen minutes from the moment he arrived.

An hour later, reporters were vying to show their press passes to the gendarme tasked with stopping the curious from invading the inn. Photographers were there too, clambering on to the tables and the chairs, taking pictures that had nothing to do with the tragedy.

As for Maigret, he received his answer from Paris over the telephone.

'The Sûreté Nationale agrees. Since you're at the scene, continue the investigation unofficially. Later today they'll send you an inspector from headquarters.'

A strange case, in short! A strange inn, too, curiously located on a sharp bend in the road. And Maigret had just learned that this was the third car in five years that had plunged into the Loing at this spot.

The other two cases were less mysterious: two cars that were speeding and hadn't anticipated the bend. Unable to straighten up in time, they had ploughed into the river. A family of five had been trapped in one of them, and in the second there had only been one victim.

And then, one Whit Sunday, a young woman suffering personal problems had drowned herself while her husband was fishing a hundred metres away, and that was how the inn got its nickname.

The Inn of the Drowned! All you had to do was go over to the telephone booth where the journalists were waiting their turn to know that before the day was out, the inn would be famous.

. . . The Mystery of the Inn of the Drowned . . . Murder at the Inn of the Drowned . . . A body in the luggage well of a twoseater convertible . . . The Mystery of the Grey Car . . .

Maigret, calm and solemn, smoked his pipe, devoured a huge ham baguette washed down with beer and absently watched the usual commotion that always hindered the police in their work.

The Inn of the Drowned

Among all these people, only two characters interested him: the owner of *La Belle Thérèse* and the lorry driver.

The bargeman had meekly sought him out.

'You know we get a bonus for speedy delivery. I should have left this morning, so, if it's possible . . .'

'Where are you going to unload?'

'Quai des Tournelles, in Paris. Another day on the canal, then not quite a day on the Seine. We'll be there the evening after tomorrow.'

Maigret made him repeat his statement:

'We'd finished eating and my wife had already gone to bed. I was about to turn in too when I heard a strange noise. From inside the boat, it's hard to tell. I put my head out of the hatch. I thought I heard a voice shouting for help.'

'What kind of voice?'

'A voice. There was the drumming of the rain on the deck, which is metal. The voice was already far off.'

'The voice of a man or of a woman?'

'More like a man!'

'How long after the first noise?'

'I wouldn't say straight away, because I had taken my shoes off, and had the time to get into my slippers.'

'Then what did you do?'

'I couldn't go outside in my slippers. I went back down. I put on my leather jacket and my shoes. I said to my wife, who was still awake: "Someone might be drowning." '

Maigret pressed him:

'Why did you think that someone might have been drowning?'

'Because when we boat people hear someone shouting for help, that's usually why! With my boathook, I've rescued more than five—'

'So, you headed over to the river?'

'I was almost there, given that it's only twenty metres between the canal and the river at that point. I saw the lights of a lorry. Then I saw a big man walking.'

'The driver. It was definitely him?'

'Yes. He told me he'd hit a car and that it had rolled into the river. I went to fetch my electric torch.'

'In other words, this went on for a while?'

'Well, yes!'

'What did the driver do in the meantime?'

'I don't know. I suppose he was trying to see something in the dark.'

'Did you go near his lorry?'

'I might have done. I don't remember. Mostly I was trying to see if a body had floated up to the surface.'

'So, you don't know whether the lorry driver was alone?'

'I assume he was. If there'd been anyone, they'd have come to help us.'

'When you realized there was nothing to be done, what did the driver say to you?'

'That he was going to inform the gendarmerie.'

'He didn't say which one?'

'No. I don't think so . . .'

'It didn't occur to you to tell him that he could

The Inn of the Drowned

telephone from the inn which is only seven hundred metres away?'

'I thought of it afterwards, when I saw him drive straight past it.'

The driver was one of those hauliers built like a strongman. He had telephoned his company to let them know that he was being detained by the police following an accident and he was calmly waiting for events to unfold, being bought drinks by the journalists in exchange for which he repeated his story over and over again.

Maigret took him to one side, into a small private dining room, where a divan suggested that the inn with the macabre name welcomed lovers.

'I thought that lorry drivers always worked in twos, especially on long-distance journeys?'

'Often, yes! A week ago my partner injured his hand and he is on sick leave, so I'm on my own.'

'What time did you leave Paris?'

'At two o'clock. I've got a mixed load and, with the roads being slippery, I couldn't go fast.'

'I presume you stopped to eat in a restaurant frequented by other lorry drivers?'

'Like you say! We have our places! We all meet at around the same time. I stopped just after Nemours, at Old Catherine's – she's a terrific cook.'

'How many lorries had pulled up there?'

'Four! Two Morin removals vans, then a petrol tanker and a rapid delivery—'

'Did you eat with the other drivers?'

'There were three of us. The others were on the next table.'

'In what order did you leave?'

'The others, I can't say. I left last because I was waiting for a call to be put through to Paris.'

'Who did you telephone?'

'The boss, to ask him to have some piston rings for me to pick up in Moulins. I'd noticed that the engine wasn't running smoothly and that the third cylinder—'

'Fine! How far behind your companions do you reckon you were?'

'I left ten minutes after the last one, which was a delivery van. Since I was going faster, it must have been four or five kilometres ahead of me.'

'And you only saw the roadster when you hit it?'

'A few metres beforehand, when it was too late to avoid it.'

'There was no light?'

'None!'

'And you didn't see anyone?'

'I can't say. It was raining. My windscreen wipers aren't too good. All I know is that, when the car was in the water, I think I saw someone in the dark trying to swim. Then I heard what sounded like a cry for help.'

'Another question: earlier, in the box under your seat, I saw an electric torch that's working perfectly. Why did you not fetch it?'

'I don't know. I was panicked. I was afraid that my lorry would slide into the Loing as well.'

The Inn of the Drowned

'When you passed the inn, were there no lights on?'

'Maybe!'

'Do you often drive this route?'

'Twice a week.'

'It didn't occur to you to telephone from the inn?'

'No! I knew that Montargis wasn't far, and I went there.'

'While you were searching by the river, could someone have hidden in your vehicle?'

'I don't think so.'

'Why not?'

'Because they'd have had to untie the ropes holding down the tarpaulin.'

'Thank you! You will of course stay here in case I need to speak to you again.'

'If that's helpful!'

His only concern was to eat and drink well, and Maigret saw him heading towards the kitchen to ask about the lunch menu.

The cook was Madame Rozier, a thin, jaundiced woman, and she was overwhelmed by such an increase in custom. Not to mention that she couldn't even grab the phone, which was being hogged by the journalists, to order supplies from the town!

A young maid, Lili, her expression too knowing for her age, joked with everyone as she served drinks, and the owner, at the bar, didn't have a free second.

It was the off season. Whereas in the summer, the inn could rely on tourists, lovers and anglers, in the autumn, the only customers were a few hunters from Paris who rented local hunting grounds and ordered their meals on set days.

Madame Rozier had said to Maigret:

'The night before last, I saw a young couple arrive in a grey car, the one that was pulled out of the river. I immediately thought that they must be newly-weds. Here's the form they filled in.'

The handwriting was pointed and shaky. It read:

Jean Vertbois, age 20, advertising broker, 18, Rue des Acacias, Paris.

The reply to the question on the form was: *Coming from Paris, going to Nice.*

Lastly, across the form, when asked to complete his companion's details, the young man had added: *And madame.*

The information had already been phoned through to Paris and inquiries were being made in Rue des Acacias, in the seventeenth arrondissement, not far from the garage where the car had been purchased.

'. . . A very pretty young woman, aged seventeen or eighteen,' the owner told Maigret. 'Between ourselves, I called her "the maiden"! She was wearing a dress that was too flimsy for the time of year and a sports jacket—'

'Did the couple have any luggage?'

'A suitcase. It's still upstairs.'

But the suitcase contained only men's clothes and underwear, which suggested that the mysterious young woman's departure had been unplanned.

'Did they seem jumpy?'

The Inn of the Drowned

'Not particularly. To be honest, they were more wrapped up in each other and they spent most of yesterday in their room. They had lunch brought up to them and Lili commented that it was awkward serving people who didn't bother to hide their passion. You get my meaning?'

'They didn't tell you why, if they were going to Nice, they stopped off less than one hundred kilometres from Paris?'

'I think they'd have stopped off anywhere, so long as they had a room.'

'What about the car?'

'It was in the garage. You've seen it. A luxury car, but several years old, the sort bought by people who don't have a lot of money. It looks expensive but costs less than a mass-produced vehicle.'

'You weren't curious enough to look inside the boot?'

'I would never take the liberty . . .'

Maigret shrugged, because the man wasn't telling him anything useful and he knew how inquisitive that kind of hotelier was.

'In short, the couple were expected to come back to the inn to sleep?'

'For dinner and to stay. We waited until ten o'clock before we cleared the table.'

'What time did the car drive out of the garage?'

'Hold on. It was already dark. At around half past four. I presumed that, after being shut up in their room for so long, our young couple fancied having some fun in

Montargis or elsewhere. The suitcase was still there, so I wasn't worried about the bill—'

'You hadn't heard anything about the accident?'

'Nothing until the gendarmes arrived at around eleven p.m.'

'And did you immediately think your guests must have been involved?'

'I feared they were. I'd noticed that the young man had had trouble getting the car out of the garage. He was clearly a novice driver. And we know about the bend close to the river.'

'Did anything in the couple's conversations arouse your suspicion?'

'I didn't listen to their conversations.'

And so, the situation could be summed up as follows:

On the Monday, at around five p.m., a certain Jean Vertbois, aged twenty, an advertising man, residing at 18 Rue des Acacias, Paris, purchased from a garage close to his home a luxury but outmoded car which he paid for with five one-thousand-franc notes. (The garage-owner, Maigret had just been informed over the telephone, had the impression that his customer's wallet contained another fairly fat wad of banknotes. Vertbois hadn't tried to negotiate the price and had said that he'd have the identity plate changed the next day. He had come to the garage alone.)

There was no information yet about Tuesday.

On the Wednesday evening, the same Vertbois arrived in his car at the Inn of the Drowned, less than one hundred kilometres from Paris, accompanied by a very

The Inn of the Drowned

young woman who seemed to be a girl from a good family, according to the innkeeper, who had excellent reasons for knowing about these things.

On the Thursday, the couple went off in the car as if going for a simple drive around the area, and a few hours later, the car, all its lights off, was hit by a lorry seven hundred metres from the inn. Both the lorry driver and a bargeman thought they heard cries for help in the darkness.

Of Jean Vertbois and the girl, there was no trace. The entire local gendarmerie had been making inquiries all day. At the railway stations, nothing! At the farms, inns and on the roads – no one matching the two descriptions.

On the other hand, the body of a very elegant, very fashionable woman in her late forties had been discovered inside the car's luggage well.

And the coroner confirmed the findings of the passing doctor, in other words that the woman had been killed on the Monday, her throat slit with a razor!

The coroner was less confident when he suggested that the body had been clumsily crammed into the luggage well only a few hours after the woman's death.

The conclusion was that when the couple had arrived at the inn, there was already a body in the car!

Did Vertbois know?

Did his young companion know?

What was their car doing by the roadside, at eight o'clock at night, with all its lights off?

Was it a breakdown that a novice driver was unable to fix? Who was in the car at that moment?

And who had shouted out in the dark?

The captain of the gendarmerie, very much a man of the world, avoided disturbing Maigret in his investigation, trying on the other hand with his team to gather as much information as possible.

Ten flat-bottomed boats went up and down the Loing searching with boathooks. Men trudged along the banks and others hunted around the weirs.

The journalists treated the inn as conquered territory and behaved as if they owned the place, filling all the rooms with their racket.

La Belle Thérèse had set off for Quai des Tournelles with its cargo of tiles, and the lorry driver, oblivious to all the fuss, was philosophical about this additional paid leave.

On the newspapers' rotary presses, the headlines were already squeezed in in bold letters; the more sensational they were, the bolder the type, and the prize went to a reporter who had written:

Two twenty-year-old lovers driving with a corpse in their boot

Then in italics:

The murky waters of the Loing engulf the murderers and their victim

It was the most trying part of the investigation, the time during which Maigret, on edge, spoke to no one, grunted, drank beers and smoked pipes, pacing like a

The Inn of the Drowned

bear in a cage. This was the period of hesitation, when all the elements gathered appear to contradict each other and, amid a jumble of intelligence, he sought in vain a common thread, worried that he might follow a lead which turned out to be a red herring.

To make things worse, the inn was draughty, and had central heating, which Maigret particularly loathed! Lastly, the food was mediocre, and the sauces were watered down to go round the many guests.

'You'll forgive me for telling you what I'm about to tell you, inspector . . .'

Captain Pillement smiled delicately as he sat down facing Maigret, who was surlier than usual.

'I know you're annoyed with me. As far as I'm concerned, I'm delighted to have detained you, because I'm beginning to believe that this road accident, so run-of-the-mill at first glance, is gradually going to turn into one of the most baffling cases imaginable.'

Maigret merely helped himself to some potato salad, sardines and beetroot, the standard hors-d'oeuvre in second-class restaurants.

'When we find out the identity of this beautiful, lovesick girl . . .'

A big car, driven by a liveried chauffeur and spattered with mud, stopped outside the inn, and a grey-haired man got out, instinctively retreating a few steps when confronted with the photographers snapping away just in case.

'Well, well!' muttered Maigret. 'I bet this is her father!'

2

Maigret had not been mistaken, but he was spared the unpleasant scene he was anticipating thanks to the remarkable dignity of the lawyer Monsieur La Pommeraye. After brushing aside the journalists in the manner of someone accustomed to asserting his authority, he'd followed Maigret into the small private lounge and introduced himself:

'Germain La Pommeraye, lawyer in Versailles.'

And his profession, like the royal town, perfectly suited his tall, aristocratic form, his olive skin, his features which barely trembled as he asked, gazing at the floor:

'Have you found her?'

'I apologize,' sighed Maigret, 'but I am going to have to ask you a number of rather specific questions.'

The lawyer waved his hand as if to say: 'Go ahead! I know how it is.'

'Can you tell me first of all what made you think that your daughter might be mixed up in this case?'

'You will understand. My daughter Viviane is seventeen and looks twenty. I say "is", but I should probably already be saying "was". She's impulsive, like her mother. And, rightly or wrongly, since being a widower, I have always refused to get in the way of her instincts. I'm not sure where she met this Jean Vertbois, but I seem to remember that it was at the swimming baths, or at a sports club whose grounds are near Boulogne.'

'Do you know Jean Vertbois personally?'

'I saw him once. My daughter, I repeat, is impulsive. One evening, she announced out of the blue: "Papa, I'm getting married!"'

Maigret rose to his feet, flung open the door, and merely glared at the journalist whose ear was glued to it.

'Continue, monsieur!'

'At first I treated it as a joke. Then, seeing she was in earnest, I asked to meet the suitor. And so, one afternoon, Jean Vertbois came to Versailles. There was one detail that displeased me at once: he had arrived in a sports car borrowed from a friend. I don't know whether you follow my drift? Young people have an absolute right to harbour ambitions, but I don't approve of a twenty-year-old cheaply satisfying a hankering for luxury, especially luxury in such poor taste . . .'

'In other words, the conversation was quite frosty?'

'To be honest, it was stormy. I asked the young man with what resources he intended to maintain a wife, and he replied with a rather disturbing openness that while he was waiting for a more brilliant position, my daughter's dowry would save her from dying of starvation. As you can see, quite the cynical little upstart, both in word and in attitude! To the extent that I wondered for a moment whether this cynicism wasn't an act that covered up a certain shyness.

'Vertbois gave a long-winded speech about the rights that parents believe that they have and on the backward thinking of a section of the bourgeoisie of which he considered me to be the perfect example.

'After an hour, I threw him out.'

'How long ago was that?' asked Maigret.

'Barely a week. When I saw my daughter afterwards, she declared that she would marry no one but Vertbois, that I didn't know him, that I'd misjudged him, and so on. And goodness me, she threatened that if I would not consent to the marriage, she would elope with him.'

'Did you stand your ground?'

'Unfortunately! I thought it was an empty threat. I believed the situation would resolve itself in time. But, since Tuesday afternoon, Viviane has vanished. On Tuesday evening, I went to Vertbois' home in Rue des Acacias, but I was told he had gone away. I spoke to the concierge, and I became convinced that he was accompanied by a very young woman, in other words, Viviane. That is why, at lunch time today, when I read about the events of last night in the newspapers . . .'

He remained calm and dignified. Little beads of sweat appeared on his forehead, however, as he said, averting his eyes:

'I ask you only one thing, inspector: to be honest! I am still tough enough to take a direct blow, but I would find it hard to cope with veering between hope and despair for any length of time. In your opinion, is my daughter alive?'

Maigret said nothing for a long while. Eventually, he muttered:

'First of all, let me ask you one last question. You appear to know your daughter very well. She seems to be totally in love with Vertbois, in both a romantic and an obsessive manner. Do you believe that if your

The Inn of the Drowned

daughter were to find out that Vertbois was a murderer, she would stand by him out of love? Don't answer too quickly. Supposing your daughter arrives at her lover's place. Forgive me but unfortunately that is the word. She learns that, in order to find the money he needed in order to elope with her, he was driven to murder.'

The two men fell silent. Eventually, Monsieur La Pommeraye sighed:

'I don't know. However, I can tell you one thing, inspector, something that no one knows. I told you earlier that I was a widower. That is true! My wife died three years ago in South America where she'd run off to with a coffee plantation owner eight years earlier. When she left, she stole one hundred thousand francs from the safe in the study. Viviane takes after her mother.'

He winced on hearing Maigret sigh:

'I hope so!'

'I beg your pardon?'

'Because if Jean Vertbois has nothing to fear from his companion, he has no reason to do away with her. If, on the other hand, for example, on discovering the body in the boot, your daughter expressed her indignation and threatened him . . .'

'I see what you mean, but I don't understand what occurred next according to the newspaper reports. At the time of the collision, the car wasn't abandoned, because the lorry driver and a bargeman heard shouts. Vertbois and Viviane had no reason to leave each other. So, it is likely . . .'

'They've been dredging the river all morning and they

haven't found anything, so far. May I ask you to come with me for a moment up to the room the couple stayed in?'

It was an ordinary room, with floral wallpaper, a brass bedstead and a mahogany mirrored wardrobe. On the washbasin shelf, a few items – a razor, a shaving brush and two toothbrushes, one of them new.

'You see,' commented Maigret. 'The man had his personal belongings with him. But the couple must have stopped on the way to buy a toothbrush for the girl and those travel slippers by the bed. I still wish I could find some evidence that it is indeed your daughter who . . .'

'Here it is!' said the father sadly, pointing to an earring glinting faintly on the rug. 'Viviane always wore those earrings, which had belonged to her mother. One of them didn't close properly. She was forever losing it and miraculously finding it again. It's this one! Now, do you still think I have a chance of finding my daughter alive?'

Maigret didn't dare reply that, if she were, Mademoiselle Viviane La Pommeraye would most likely be charged with being complicit in a murder!

He'd had to persuade the lawyer to return to Versailles and, in the continuing downpour, the Inn of the Drowned increasingly resembled a police headquarters.

Tired of standing in the rain watching the operations of the bargemen probing the river, some journalists were philosophically playing *belote*. The captain of the gendarmerie had put his car at the disposal of Maigret, who declined to use it and whose inconsistent activity did not inspire confidence in those who were unfamiliar with his methods.

And so, when they saw him go into the telephone booth, the reporters imagined that they were about to learn something new and, eavesdroppers by profession, they shamelessly lurked by the door.

But Maigret was calling the Paris Observatory, asking first of all for the latest weather forecast and insisting on certain details.

'You say there was no moon last night at around eight p.m.? Will it be the same tonight? . . . Pardon? The moon rises at twelve minutes past midnight? . . . Thank you . . .'

He came out looking extremely pleased! He even took a perverse pleasure in saying to the journalists:

'Gentlemen, here's some good news: we're in for at least three days of torrential rain.'

Next, he could be seen having a long conversation with Captain Pillement, who then disappeared and was gone for the rest of the day.

There was heavy drinking. Someone had discovered a Vouvray which they all wanted, and Lili, going from table to table, encountered wandering hands which she didn't push away too fiercely.

When darkness fell, at half past four, that put an end to the search in the Loing and it became unlikely that a body or bodies would be found, because the current would have swept them into the Seine by now.

To clear the road, a breakdown vehicle had taken away the car salvaged from the river and driven it to

Montagis where it was delivered into the hands of the police.

It was six o'clock when a reporter called the innkeeper over and said:

'What's on the menu for dinner?'

And a voice replied:

'Nothing at all!'

Not least surprised was the owner, who was trying to see who had answered in his place, especially in such a rude, unbusinesslike manner. It was Maigret, who was calmly walking across the room.

'As a matter of fact, gentlemen, I'm going to ask you not to dine here this evening. I am not banning you from coming back at around ten p.m. if you like, or even from staying the night at the inn. But between seven and nine p.m., I very much want only the people who were here last night to be on the premises.'

'Reconstruction?' shouted one smart alec.

'Not quite! I warn you right away that there's no point hanging around nearby, because you won't see anything. But, if you behave, you will probably have a sensational article for your morning editions tomorrow . . .'

'At what time?'

'Let's say by eleven. I know a place in Montargis where you can eat wonderfully well: the Hôtel de la Cloche. Go there, all of you. Tell the owner that I sent you and you'll be well looked after. When I come and join you—'

'Aren't you eating with us?'

'I'm invited elsewhere, but I shan't be long. Now, it's

The Inn of the Drowned

take it or leave it, and if anyone tries to be clever, I guarantee he won't obtain the tiniest scrap of information. See you later, gentlemen and *bon appétit!*'

After they'd left, he breathed more easily, and he darted the furious owner a roguish glance.

'Come on! You make your money on the booze not on the food. And they've been drinking all day.'

'They'd have carried on!'

'Listen to me! It is essential that, between seven and ten p.m., everyone in the inn must be where they were yesterday, that the lighting is the same.'

'That's quite simple.'

There was someone they seemed to have forgotten – Joseph Lecoin, the lorry driver. He was watching Maigret in amazement, and finally he opened his mouth.

'What about me?'

'You are going to drive me to Nemours.'

'In the lorry?'

'Yes, why not? For want of a chauffeur-driven limousine . . .'

'As you wish. If I can be of help . . .'

And that was how Inspector Maigret left the Inn of the Drowned sitting in a ten-tonne lorry that made an infernal racket.

3

'Where shall I drop you off?'

They had driven in silence, in the dark and the rain, meeting the occasional car that dipped its headlights, with the windscreen wiper making a humming sound like a giant bumblebee.

'You're not dropping me off, my friend!'

The driver looked at his companion in bewilderment, thinking he was joking:

'So, what then? Are we going back to Paris?'

'No! Let me check the time.'

Maigret had to hit the cigarette lighter to see his watch, whose hands showed half past seven.

'Good! Stop at the first drinking den you see. There's no hurry.'

And Maigret turned up the collar of his overcoat to cross the street, leaned familiarly on the counter of a small bar in the company of Lecoin, who was taken aback at the change in Maigret's attitude.

Not that he had become threatening, or that he was giving vent to his ill humour in any way!

It was quite the opposite. He was calm. Sometimes, it even seemed his eyes were laughing. He was self-assured and, if anyone had asked him, he would have readily replied:

'Life is beautiful!'

He enjoyed his drink, checked his watch again, paid the bill and announced:

'Let's go!'

'Where are we off to?'

'First of all, for dinner at Old Catherine's, as you did last night. You see! It's raining just as hard. And this is exactly the same time.'

Only three lorries indicated the location of the inn,

The Inn of the Drowned

whose exterior was particularly modest, but the long-distance drivers knew they would find tasty casseroles simmering away inside. The owner served the food herself, helped by her fourteen-year-old daughter.

'Well, hello? You're back?' she asked in surprise on seeing Lecoin enter.

He shook the other drivers' hands and sat down in a corner with Maigret.

'Supposing we have the same as you had yesterday?' suggested Maigret.

'There's not a huge choice here. You have to have the day's special. Look! It's veal fricandeau with a sorrel sauce.'

'One of my favourite dishes.'

Had there not been, in the past few minutes, a certain change in the burly lorry driver's behaviour? His mood was less open. He kept glancing covertly at Maigret and was probably wondering what the police inspector was playing at.

'Get a move on, Catherine. Some of us are in a hurry.'

'You always say that, and then you sit around for a quarter of an hour drinking your coffee.'

The fricandeau was perfect, and the coffee much better than that usually served in bars. Every so often, Maigret would take his watch from his pocket and seemed to be waiting for the other drivers to leave with a certain impatience.

At last, they got up, after a round of vintage marc, and shortly afterwards the thrum of engines could be heard.

'Marc for me too,' Maigret ordered.

And to Lecoin:

'This is exactly how things were yesterday, is it not?'

'Absolutely. This would be the time to leave. At this hour, I'd already made my telephone—'

'Let's go!'

'Are we going back there?'

'Just like yesterday. Does that bother you?'

'Me? Why would it bother me? Seeing as I have nothing to hide . . .'

But just then, Catherine came over and asked the driver:

'Tell me! Did you give my message to Benoît?'

'Of course I did. It's sorted!'

Once in the lorry, Maigret asked:

'Who is Benoît?'

'He has a petrol pump in Montargis. He's a pal. I always stop at his place to fill up. Old Catherine would like a pump to be installed at her place too, and I was to tell Benoît—'

'It's bucketing down, isn't it!'

'Even a bit more than yesterday. Just think! When you have to drive all night through this downpour . . .'

'Are we not going too fast?'

'Just like yesterday.'

Maigret lit his pipe.

'Us lorry drivers,' muttered Lecoin, 'we're always the ones that people yell at because we hog the middle of the road, or we don't pull over fast enough. But if the people who drive small cars had to steer beasts like ours . . .'

Suddenly, a curse and Lecoin braked sharply, so

The Inn of the Drowned

sharply that Maigret almost went headfirst into the windscreen.

'Well, blow me down!' exclaimed Joseph Lecoin.

And he looked at his companion, frowned and grumbled:

'Was it you who had it positioned there?'

There was indeed a car, at the exact spot where the lorry had crashed into Jean Vertbois' convertible the previous night. A grey car, like the other one! It was raining! The night was dark! The car had no lights!

And yet, the lorry had come to a halt more than three metres from it!

For a split second, the driver's face had betrayed a mounting anger, but he merely grumbled:

'You could have warned me. Supposing I hadn't seen it in time . . .'

'And yet we were chatting.'

'So what?'

'Yesterday, you were alone. So you were fully concentrated on the road.'

And Lecoin asked with a shrug:

'What do you want now?'

'We're going to get down. Over here. Wait. I want to try an experiment. Shout for help.'

'Me?'

'Since those who shouted yesterday aren't here, someone has to take their place.'

And reluctantly Lecoin shouted, sensing a trap.

His anxiety redoubled when he heard footsteps and a shape moved in the darkness.

'Come closer!' Maigret called out to the newcomer.

It was the bargeman from *La Belle Thérèse*, whom Maigret had asked the gendarmerie to summon back, without letting on to anyone.

'Well?'

'It is difficult to state categorically. But for me, it was more or less the same thing.'

'What?' groaned Lecoin.

'I don't know who shouted, but I'd say it was more or less the same sound as last night.'

This time, the giant was on the verge of losing his composure and setting upon the bargeman, who was unaware of the part he was playing in the charade.

'Get back into the lorry!'

Someone was coming towards them, who had not budged until then – Captain Pillement.

'Everything's fine!' Maigret told him in a hushed tone. 'As for the rest, we'll soon see . . .'

And he clambered back into the cab next to Lecoin, who was no longer trying to be amiable.

'What do I do?'

'As you did yesterday!'

'Do I go to Montargis?'

'As you did yesterday!'

'As you wish! I don't know what you've got in mind, but if you think I'm mixed up in this business . . .'

They were already passing the Inn of the Drowned, where four windows were lit up, one of them displaying the telephone number in enamel lettering.

'So it didn't occur to you to stop and telephone?'

The Inn of the Drowned

'I already told you.'

'Keep going!'

Silence! A sullen man, making abrupt movements, and Maigret, smoking his pipe in his dark corner!

They arrived in Montargis, and suddenly Maigret said:

'You've gone past it.'

'What?'

'The gendarmerie.'

'That's you, with all this messing me about.'

He wanted to reverse, because the gendarmerie was only fifty metres away.

'No! No!' protested Maigret. 'Carry on!'

'Carry on what?'

'Doing exactly what you did yesterday.'

'But I went—'

'You didn't go directly to the gendarmerie. The proof is that the time doesn't tally. Where is Benoît's petrol pump?'

'At the second junction.'

'Let's go there!'

'What for?'

'Nothing. Do as I tell you.'

It was an ordinary pump, in front of a bicycle shop. The place wasn't lit up, but through the windows a kitchen could be seen where shadows were moving around.

The lorry had barely stopped when a man came out of the kitchen. He had clearly heard the sound of the engine and the squeal of the brakes.

'How many litres?' he asked, without a glance at the lorry.

A moment later, he recognized it and looked up at Lecoin, asking:

'What are you doing here? I thought—'

'Give me fifty litres!'

Maigret stayed in his corner, invisible to the petrol-pump owner. Benoît, believing himself to be alone with his friend, would perhaps say something, but Lecoin, sensing the danger, hurriedly said:

'So, inspector, is that all you require?'

'Oh! You've got someone with you?'

'Someone from the police who's doing a reconstruction, as he calls it. I don't understand a thing. It's always the little people they bother, whereas . . .'

Maigret had jumped down and gone into the shop, much to the surprise of the bicycle seller. That was because he'd spotted the man's wife in the backroom.

'Lecoin is asking how it's all going,' he asked on the off chance.

She gave him a wary look, leaned over to look out of the shop window and asked:

'Is Lecoin here?'

'He's filling up.'

'They haven't given him any trouble?'

And, worried, baffled by the intrusion of the man in a bowler hat, she headed towards the doorway.

You couldn't see clearly. It took an effort to make out the features on people's faces.

'Hey, Paul . . .'

That was her husband, encumbered by the petrol hose.

'Is that Lecoin there?'

The Inn of the Drowned

Maigret unhurriedly filled his pipe and lit it, taking advantage of the shelter afforded by the shop, illuminating for a moment the nickel-plated handlebars of the bicycles.

'Are you coming, Paul?'

Then Maigret clearly heard one of the two men ask the other:

'What do we do?'

Just in case, he grabbed his revolver, which he kept in his pocket, ready to shoot through the fabric if necessary. The street was deserted, unlit. And Lecoin was powerful enough to floor any adversary with a single punch.

'What would *you* do?'

The woman was still in the doorway, hunching her shoulders because of the cold. Joseph Lecoin, clambering down heavily from his seat, took a couple of uncertain steps forward.

'Supposing we all go inside and talk?' suggested Maigret calmly.

Benoît hung up his petrol hose. Lecoin, who still hadn't made up his mind, screwed the cap back on to his petrol tank.

In the end, he was the one who grunted as he walked towards the entrance to the shop:

'This isn't what was agreed. After you, inspector.'

4

It was a typical tradesman's cottage, with its carved oak dresser, a gingham oilcloth on the table and ugly pink and mauve things won at a fairground serving as vases.

'Have a seat,' mumbled the woman, automatically wiping the table in front of Maigret.

And Benoît took a bottle from the dresser, four small glasses which he filled without saying a word, while Lecoin sat astride a chair facing backwards, resting his elbows on the back.

'Did you suspect something?' he asked, looking Maigret in the eyes.

'Yes, for two reasons: number one, because we heard only a man's shouts, which was strange given that there was a girl at the scene and that, had she been in difficulty, she was a good enough swimmer to stay afloat for a while and call for help. And then, after an accident like that, a person doesn't drive twenty kilometres to inform the gendarmerie when there's a telephone close by. The windows of the inn were lit up. It was impossible not to think of—'

'That's right,' admitted Lecoin. 'He was the one who wanted—'

'He'd climbed into the lorry, of course?'

It was too late to back down. Besides, the two men had made their decision while the woman looked relieved. She was the one who urged:

'It's best to tell him everything. It's not for two measly thousand-franc notes that we have to—'

'Joseph will explain,' said her husband.

And after downing the contents of his glass, Lecoin began:

The Inn of the Drowned

'Let's say that everything happened just as it did last night. You were right. In spite of the rain and my defective windscreen wiper, I have good eyesight and good enough brakes not to crash into a stationary vehicle on the road. So I stopped one and a half metres from it. I thought it had broken down and I got down to lend a hand. That was when I saw a distraught young man who asked me if I wanted to earn two thousand francs—'

'By helping him to push the car into the water?' Maigret broke in.

'He could probably have pushed it in by himself. That's what he was trying to do when I arrived. But what he wanted most was to be driven somewhere that no one would ever find out about. I think that if it had been only him, I'd never have agreed. But there was the girl—'

'Was she still alive?'

'Of course! To persuade me, he told me that they weren't being allowed to marry, that they loved each other, and they wanted to fake a suicide to stop anyone from trying to find them and separate them. I don't like those kinds of scheme, but if you'd seen that poor kid in the rain . . . In short, I helped push the car into the Loing. The two youngsters hid in my lorry. They asked me to shout for help, for the sake of credibility, which I did. That way, people would think that the pair of them had died. Then all I had to do was drive them to Montargis.

'I gathered, on the way, that the young man wasn't stupid. He knew he couldn't go to a hotel. Nor did he want to take a train. He asked me if I knew anyone who, for another two thousand francs, they could stay with for a few days, until the investigation was over. I thought of . . .'

The woman confirmed:

'We also believed they were lovers. So, seeing as our brother-in-law has his room here and he's off on military service—'

'Are they still in the house?'

'Not her.'

'What?'

And Maigret looked about him with concern.

'After lunch,' began the garage-owner, 'when I saw the newspaper, I went upstairs and asked if the story of the body was true. The girl tore the paper from my hands, skimmed it and suddenly she shot through the open door and bolted.'

'Without a coat?'

'Without a coat or hat.'

'What about the young man?'

'He swore he didn't understand a thing, that he'd just bought the car and he hadn't had the curiosity to look inside the luggage well.'

'Is this the only door to your house?'

Just then, while the bicycle seller was shaking his head in reply, they heard a commotion in the street. Maigret ran outside and found a form lying on the ground, a young man struggling, trying in vain to run away, despite the leg he'd broken jumping from the upstairs.

It was both dramatic and pathetic, because Vertbois was wild with rage and would not yet admit he was beaten.

The Inn of the Drowned

'If you come any closer, I'll shoot.'

Maigret jumped on him, and Vertbois did not shoot, either because he was afraid, or because he lacked the nerve.

'Calm down, now.'

The young man cursed the driver, the garage-owner and his wife and accused them of betraying him.

He was the classic deviant, several dozen examples of which Maigret, sadly, had already been able to study – sneaky, envious, so greedy for pleasure and money that he would stop at nothing.

'Where is Viviane?' Maigret asked as he handcuffed him.

'I don't know.'

'So, you managed to convince her that you were pushing the car into the water purely to have people believe in a lovers' suicide pact?'

'She wouldn't let me out of her sight.'

'And that's a nuisance, isn't it, being in possession of a body that you can't get rid of!'

The odious crime in all its stupidity, all its horror, the crime that never pays!

Jean Vertbois, seeing that his marriage plans had failed and that La Pommeraye's money was eluding him, even if he kidnapped Viviane, had gone for a mistress of a certain age, whom he had been with for a long time, lured her to his place, killed her, stolen her money and bought a cheap car with some of that cash, planning to dispose of the body in a deserted place.

But then Viviane appeared, with her youthful love,

her passion. Viviane determined never to go back home and to share her lover's fate.

She was glued to him! The hours went by, the car kept going, still with the body in it.

Viviane believed she was on a real honeymoon, whereas she was deep in a horrendous drama!

She embraced the man she loved, while he only thought of the grisly bundle he had to get rid of at all costs!

That was when, in desperation, he came up with the idea of this fake suicide, which was complicated but also facilitated by the unexpected arrival of a lorry.

'The information you promised, inspector?'

At La Cloche, the journalists had tucked into a meal that was a veritable banquet and were in a relaxed mood.

'Marthe Dorval's killer is in hospital.'

'Marthe Dorval?'

'A former operetta singer, who had savings and was the mistress of Jean Vertbois.'

'He's in hospital?'

'In Montargis hospital with a broken leg. I give you permission to go and photograph him and to ask him any questions you like.'

'What about the girl?'

Maigret bowed his head. He had no news of her, and she may have committed an act of desperation.

It was gone midnight, and Maigret was at the Nemours police station with Captain Pillement, with whom he was discussing the events, when the telephone rang.

The Inn of the Drowned

The captain, who had picked it up, looked pleasantly surprised and asked a few questions: 'Are you certain of the address? . . . Listen! As a precaution, bring me the driver . . . Too bad if he's drunk . . .'

And he explained to Maigret:

'My men have just found a taxi driver from Montargis who during the day picked up a girl wearing no coat and no hat. She had him drive her into the countryside, near Bourges, where she went into an isolated manor house. Seeing that his customer wasn't even carrying a handbag, the driver was worried about his payment, but she told him several times: "My aunt will pay."'

And indeed, Viviane La Pommeraye, shattered, desperate, had taken refuge at the home of one of her aunts where she'd spent her holidays since her childhood.

Madame Maigret's Suitor

I

Like most families, the Maigrets had various traditions that eventually took on as much importance as religious rituals did for others.

For the many years that they had lived on Place des Vosges, in summer, as soon as he set foot on the staircase from the courtyard, Maigret had been in the habit of unknotting his dark tie, which gave him the time to climb up to the first floor.

From that point, the staircase of the apartment building, a former luxurious private residence like all those around the square, no longer rose majestically with a wrought-iron railing and imitation marble walls but became steep and narrow, and Maigret reached the second floor slightly out of breath with his detachable collar undone.

He then had to follow the ill-lit passageway to his door, the third on the left and, as he inserted his key in the lock, his jacket slung over his arm, he would shout a traditional:

'It's me!'

And he'd sniff the air, guessing what was for lunch

Madame Maigret's Suitor

from the aroma, walk into the dining room, whose tall window was open onto the magnificent sight of the small gardens below, with their four fountains.

It was June. The weather was particularly hot, and the entire Police Judiciaire could talk of nothing but holidays. Sometimes, out in the street, men could be seen with their jackets over their arms, while beer flowed freely at all the café terraces.

'Have you seen your suitor?' asked Maigret, standing in front of the window and mopping his brow.

At that moment, no one would have guessed that in the crime-fighting laboratory that is the Police Judiciaire he had just spent hours and hours delving into the darkest and most dismal recesses of the human soul.

Outside his work, he found the slightest trifle amusing, especially when it was a matter of teasing gullible Madame Maigret. For the past two weeks, the running joke had been asking for news of her suitor.

'Did he do his two little laps of honour around the square? Still as mysterious and distinguished? When I think that you have a soft spot for distinguished gentlemen, yet you married me!'

Madame Maigret bustled about setting the table, because she didn't want a maid and was content with a cleaning woman in the mornings for the heavy housework. She entered into the banter.

'I didn't say he was distinguished!'

'But you described him to me: pearl-grey brimmed hat, little upturned moustache, probably dyed, walking stick with a carved ivory pommel.'

'You can laugh! Sooner or later, you'll realize that I'm the one who's right. I maintain that he's no ordinary man and that his behaviour is definitely a cover for something important.'

From the window, you could absently watch the comings and goings across the gardens, which were quite empty in the mornings, but in the afternoons the benches were filled with local mothers and maids keeping a watchful eye on the children playing.

Around the small park, which, with its girdle of railings, is one of the most classic Paris garden squares, the buildings are all the same, with their arcades and steeply sloping slate roofs.

At first, Madame Maigret had paid scant attention to the stranger, who could hardly go unnoticed, because everything about his appearance and his demeanour was around twenty or thirty years out of date and he was like a caricature in a comic magazine.

It was early in the morning, the hour when the windows were open and you could see servants in the apartments busy with the housework.

'He seems to be looking for something!' Madame Maigret commented.

In the afternoon, she had gone to visit her sister and the next day, at exactly the same time, she saw her stranger again. He was walking around the gardens at a steady pace, once, twice, before finally disappearing in the direction of Place de la République.

'No doubt a fellow who's fond of young housemaids and comes to watch them shaking out the rugs!' Maigret had said when his wife, chatting about this and that, had mentioned her elderly beau.

That afternoon, she hadn't been particularly surprised to see him at three o'clock, sitting absolutely still on a bench, just opposite her window, both hands clasping the pommel of his walking stick.

At four o'clock, he was still there. And at five o'clock. Only close to six o'clock did he get up and amble off down Rue des Tournelles, without having spoken a word to anyone, without even unfolding a newspaper.

'Don't you find that curious, Maigret?'

Because Madame Maigret had always called her husband by his surname.

'I already told you: there must have been some pretty little housemaids nearby.'

And the next day, Madame Maigret raised the subject again:

'I watched him closely, because again he sat there on the same bench for three hours.'

'Fancy that! Maybe it was to gaze at you! From that bench it must be possible to see into our apartment, and this gentleman is in love with you.'

'Don't talk nonsense!'

'First of all, he uses a walking stick and you've always liked men who walk with a cane. I bet he wears a pince-nez.'

'Why?'

'Because you have a fondness for men who wear a pince-nez!'

They gently teased each other, after twenty years

of marriage, savouring the peace and quiet of their interior.

'Listen, I paid close attention to the people around him. There was indeed a maid, just opposite him, on a chair. I'd already noticed her at the greengrocer's, first of all because she's very pretty, and secondly because she looks classy.'

'There you are!' crowed Maigret. 'Your classy servant was sitting opposite the old gent. Have you noticed how women sometimes sit down without paying much heed to the eyeful they're presenting, and your beau spent the afternoon ogling her.'

'You have a one-track mind!'

'Until I see your mystery man.'

'Can I help it if he doesn't come at times when you're here?'

And Maigret, who was involved in so many dramatic events, re-immersed himself in this gentle ribbing, never forgetting to ask for news of the man who had become, in their language, Madame Maigret's suitor.

'You can laugh all you like! Even so, there is something about him, I don't know what it is, that intrigues me and scares me a little. I can't explain. When you look at him, it's hard to take your eyes off him. He's capable of sitting there for hours on end, absolutely still, and his pupils don't even move behind his pince-nez.'

'You've seen his pupils from here?'

Madame Maigret almost blushed, as if caught out.

'I went to have a closer look. Most of all I wanted to know whether you were right. Well, the blonde maid, who always has two children in tow, acts very respectably and there's nothing to see.'

'Does she also stay there all afternoon?'

'She arrives at around three o'clock, usually after the man. She always has a piece of crochet work with her. They leave at around the same time. She works at her crocheting for hours on end, without looking up, other than to call the children back from time to time when they stray too far.'

'Do you not think, darling, that in the Paris squares, there are hundreds of maids who crochet or knit for hours on end while keeping an eye on their charges?'

'It's possible!'

'And scores of old men of private means who have nothing better to do than soak up the sun and lust after pretty girls?'

'This one isn't old.'

'You told me yourself that his moustache was probably dyed and that he must be wearing a wig.'

'Yes, but he doesn't look old.'

'The same age as me?'

'Sometimes he looks older, and sometimes younger.'

And Maigret, pretending to be jealous, grumbled:

'One of these days, I'll have to come and look this suitor of yours in the face.'

He was no more serious about it than Madame Maigret. In a similar way, once before they had taken an amused interest in two lovers who met up every night under the arcades, their arguments and reconciliations, until the day when the girl, who was a servant at the dairy, had met up with a different young man in exactly the same spot.

'You know, Maigret . . .'

'What?'

'I've been thinking. I wonder whether that man isn't there to spy on someone.'

The days passed and the sun grew hotter and hotter; in the evenings, the gardens were increasingly crowded, filled with craftsmen from the neighbouring streets who came for a breath of fresh air around the four fountains.

'What I find odd is that in the mornings, he never sits down. And why does he walk around the square twice, as if he were waiting for a signal?'

'What is your pretty blonde maid doing at that time?'

'I don't see her. She works in a house on the right, and from here you can't see what's going on inside. I run into her at the market, where she speaks to no one except to tell the stallholders what she wants. She never bargains, so she gets swindled by at least twenty per cent. She always looks as if her mind is elsewhere.'

'Well, next time I have a delicate surveillance mission, I'll give it to you instead of my men.'

'You can laugh! We'll see one of these days whether . . .'

It was eight o'clock. Maigret had already had dinner, which was rare, because he was usually detained at Quai des Orfèvres until quite late.

He was leaning on the window-sill in his shirt-sleeves, pipe between his teeth, staring vaguely at the pink sky

Madame Maigret's Suitor

where dusk was gathering, at Place des Vosges filled with people made languid by the early summer.

Behind him, he could hear the clatter that signalled Madame Maigret was putting away the dishes and would soon join him with a piece of needlework.

Evenings like this, without a thorny case to solve, a murderer to track down or a thief to watch, evenings when his thoughts could wander peacefully in the rosy glow of the sky, were rare, and perhaps Maigret had never enjoyed his pipe so much, when all of a sudden, without turning around, he called out:

'Henriette?'

'Do you want something?'

'Come and see.'

With the stem of his pipe, he pointed to a bench, just opposite them. On the corner of this bench, an old vagrant-like fellow was grabbing some shut-eye. In the other corner . . .

'That's him!' declared Madame Maigret. 'Fancy that!'

She found it almost improper that 'her' afternoon stroller should have departed from his routine and be sitting on the bench at that hour.

'He appears to have fallen asleep,' muttered Maigret, relighting his pipe. 'If there weren't two flights of stairs to climb back up, I'd go and have a closer look, just to find out what stuff he's made of, this beau of yours.'

Madame Maigret went back into her kitchen. Maigret watched three boys having an argument. They ended up grappling in the dirt, while others roller-skated around them.

His second pipe had already gone out and Maigret was still in the same position, the stranger too, while the vagrant had woken and was plodding towards the banks of the Seine. Madame Maigret settled down, a piece of sewing on her knees – ever the housewife incapable of sitting idle for an hour.

'Is he still there?'

'Yes.'

'Aren't they about to lock the gates?'

'In a few minutes. The warden is starting to shepherd people towards the exits.'

But the warden somehow didn't see the stranger, who still hadn't moved, and three of the gates were already locked. He was about to turn the key in the lock of the fourth when Maigret, without saying a word, picked up his jacket and went downstairs.

From up above, Madame Maigret saw him talking to the man in green, who took his job as warden very seriously. But he eventually allowed Maigret in, and he marched straight over to the man with the pince-nez.

Madame Maigret had risen. She could tell that something was wrong, and she made a sign to her husband that meant:

'Is that it?'

She couldn't have said what, but for days and days she had been fearing something would happen. Maigret nodded, posted the warden by the gate and went back home.

'My collar, my tie.'

'Is he dead?'

'As dead as a doornail! For at least two hours, or I don't know my job.'

'Do you think he had a stroke?'

Silence from Maigret who always struggled to knot his tie.

'What are you going to do?'

'Begin the investigation, of course! Inform the public prosecutor, the coroner and the rest of them.'

A velvety darkness had fallen over the gardens, where the music of the fountains had intensified. The fourth, always the same, had a sharper sound than the others.

A few moments later, Maigret went into the tobacconist's in Rue du Pas-de-la-Mule, made a series of telephone calls, found a police officer and posted him by the gate in place of the warden.

Madame Maigret did not want to go downstairs. She knew that her husband hated her meddling in his cases. She also understood that, for once, he was relaxed, because no one had noticed the dead man with the pince-nez, or his own comings and goings.

The square, furthermore, was almost empty. Only the florists downstairs were sitting in front of their doorway, and the owner of the car accessories shop, in long grey overalls, had gone over to chat with them.

They were surprised to see a first car stop in front of the gate and go into the gardens; they eventually wandered over when they saw a second car and a solemn gentleman, who must have been from the public prosecutor's office. Finally, when the ambulance arrived, the group of curious onlookers had swelled to around fifty people, but no one suspected the reason for this strange gathering because the shrubs concealed the main stage.

Madame Maigret had not switched on the lights: she often kept them off when she was alone. She was still looking out over the square and saw windows opening, but there was no sign of the pretty blonde maid.

The ambulance left first, heading for the Forensic Institute.

Then a car, with several passengers.

Then Maigret, on the pavement, spoke for a few minutes with some gentlemen before crossing the road and going back up to his apartment.

'Aren't you putting the lights on?' he grumbled, trying to see in the dark.

She turned the button.

'Close the window. It's not warm.'

This was no longer the relaxed Maigret of earlier, but the Maigret of the Police Judiciaire, whose bouts of ill temper made the young inspectors quake.

'Stop sewing! You're getting on my nerves! Can't you be still for a moment without your needlework in your hands?'

She stopped sewing. He paced up and down the small apartment, his hands behind his back, occasionally darting strange looks at his wife.

'Why did you say he sometimes seemed young and sometimes old?'

'I don't know. It was an impression. Why? How old is he?'

'He's not even thirty.'

Madame Maigret's Suitor

'What are you saying?'

'I'm saying that your fellow is not at all what he seemed. I'm saying that beneath his wig he had fair hair, that his moustache was fake and that he wore a kind of corset that made him as stiff as an old man.'

'But . . .'

'There are no buts. I'm still wondering by what miracle you somehow sniffed out this case.'

He almost held her responsible for what had happened, for their ruined evening, for the workload ahead.

'You know what's going on, don't you? Well, your suitor was murdered, on that bench.'

'That's not possible! In front of all those people?'

'In front of all those people, yes, and most likely at precisely the moment when there were the most people.'

'Do you think that that maid . . . ?'

'I have just sent the bullet to an expert, who should be phoning me in a few minutes.'

'How could someone have fired a shot and . . .'

Maigret shrugged and waited for the telephone call that was not long in coming.

'Hello! . . . Yes, that's what I thought too . . . But I needed your confirmation . . .'

Madame Maigret was impatient, but he deliberately took his time, grunting, as if it were none of her business:

'Air rifle, a special model, extremely rare.'

'I don't understand.'

'It means that the fellow was killed from a distance, by someone lying in wait at one of the windows who was able to take all the time they needed to aim . . . What is more, the killer is a first-class marksman, because he shot him directly in the heart, causing instant death.'

'And so, in the sunshine, while the crowds . . .'

Her nerves frayed, Madame Maigret suddenly began to cry:

'I'm sorry. I can't help it. I feel as if it's somehow my fault. It's silly, but . . .'

'When you've pulled yourself together, I'll take a witness statement from you.'

'Me? A witness?'

'Of course! So far, you are the only person who is able to give any useful information, since your curiosity drove you to . . .'

And Maigret was willing to divulge some details, but still as if talking to himself.

'The man had no papers on him. Pockets almost empty apart from a few hundred-franc notes, a little change, a tiny key and a nail file. We're still going to try to identify him.'

'Thirty years old!' echoed Madame Maigret.

It was disconcerting! And she now understood the almost mesmerizing effect created by this young man frozen in the attitudes of an old man, like a waxwork figure.

'Are you ready?'

'Go ahead!'

'Please note that I am questioning you in the line of duty and that tomorrow I will have to write a report on this interview.'

Madame Maigret smiled, a wan smile, because she was intimidated.

'Did you notice this man today?'

'I didn't see him in the morning because I went to Les Halles. In the afternoon, he was in his usual place.'

'What about the blonde maid?'

'She was there too, as always.'

'Had you ever seen them speaking to each other?'

'They would have had to raise their voices, because they were more than eight metres apart.'

'And they stayed like that, without moving, all afternoon?'

'Except that the woman was crocheting.'

'Always crochet? For two weeks?'

'Yes . . .'

'Did you notice what crochet stitch it was?'

'No. Had it been knitting, I know all about that, but—'

'What time did the woman leave?'

'I don't know. I was busy making custard. Probably at around five o'clock, as usual.'

'And in the opinion of the coroner, death did indeed occur at around five p.m. Only now it's a question of minutes. Did the woman leave before or after five o'clock, before or after the death? I wonder why today of all days, you needed to make custard. When you're spying on people, you see it through to the end, conscientiously!'

'Do you think that woman—?'

'I don't think! I just know that your information is the only basis I have for my investigation, and it is not brilliant. Do you even know who she works for, this blonde maidservant?'

'She always goes into 17A.'

'And who lives at 17A?'

'I don't know that either. People who have a big American car and a driver who looks foreign.'

'Is that all you noticed? Well, you'd make a fine police officer, I can tell you! A big American car and a driver who . . .'

This was just a show he put on when he was embarrassed, and his brief outburst ended up in a broad smile.

'You know, old girl, that if you hadn't been intrigued by your suitor's little game, I would be in real trouble right now? I'm not saying that the situation is great, or that the investigation will go smoothly, but there is something to go on, slender though it is.'

'The beautiful blonde?'

'The beautiful blonde, as you call her! That reminds me . . .'

He dashed over to the telephone and alerted an inspector whom he put on sentry duty outside number 17A, instructing him that if a beautiful blonde girl came out, he was not to lose sight of her whatever happened.

'And now, to bed. There'll be time tomorrow morning.'

He was dozing off when his wife's timid voice ventured:

'Don't you think it would be wise to—'

'No, no and no!' he shouted, half sitting up in bed. 'Just because you had a feeling something wasn't right, that doesn't mean you should start giving me advice! To start with, it's time to go to sleep.'

It was the hour when the slate roofs of Place des Vosges glinted silver in the moonlight and the four fountains continued to play a sort of chamber music, with the fourth always hurried and sounding a discordant note.

2

When Maigret, his face smeared with lather, his braces dangling down his thighs, first glanced out at Place des Vosges, there was already a large crowd around the bench where, the previous evening, a body had been discovered.

The florist, better informed than the others, because she had watched the arrival of the public prosecutor, was giving voluble explanations and, even from a distance, it was clear from her categorical stance that she was certain of her opinions.

The entire neighbourhood was there, and passers-by who a little earlier had been rushing to arrive on time at their workshop or office suddenly had time to stop, because it was a matter of a murder.

'Do you know that woman over there?' Maigret asked, pointing with the tip of his razor at a youngish woman wearing a very elegant, light-coloured English suit that made her stand out from her neighbours.

'I've never seen her. At least, I don't think so.'

That meant nothing. The first floors of the apartment buildings on Place des Vosges were occupied by wealthy upper-class and society people. All the same, a woman from the milieu that Maigret was grumpily studying was rarely out and about at eight o'clock in the morning, unless it was to walk her dog.

'Right! This morning, you're going to buy lots of food. You'll go into every shop. You'll listen to what people are saying and, most importantly, you'll try to find out about your blonde maid and her employers.'

'This time you won't accuse me of being a gossip!' teased Madame Maigret. 'When do you expect to be home?'

'How do I know?'

Because, although he had slept that night, the investigation had nevertheless continued, and he hoped to find some concrete evidence on his arrival at Quai des Orfèvres.

At eleven p.m. Doctor Hébrard, the renowned coroner, who was attending an opening night at the Comédie Française in a frock coat, had received a message. He'd stayed until the final act then gone to the dressing room of one of the actresses, who was a friend of his, to congratulate her and, fifteen minutes later, at the Forensic Institute, which was no other than the new mortuary, an assistant had handed him his white coat, while another removed the refrigerated body of the Place des Vosges victim from one of the storage units lining the walls.

Meanwhile, under the eaves of the Palais de Justice, in the Records department where the files of all the criminals of France and most of the criminals around the world are kept, two men in grey overalls were patiently comparing fingerprints.

Not far away, separated by a spiral staircase, the experts on night duty at the laboratory were embarking on their painstaking task of examining various items: a dark suit of an old-fashioned cut, button boots, a rush cane with a carved ivory pommel, a wig, a pince-nez and a tuft of the dead man's fair hair.

After shaking hands with his colleagues and exchanging a few brief words with the chief, Maigret walked into his office, which smelled of stale pipe smoke despite the open window, where he found three reports waiting for him in different coloured folders, neatly arranged on his desk.

Doctor Hébrard's report first: the victim had apparently died almost instantaneously after being shot from a distance of more than twenty metres, perhaps a hundred, with a small-calibre but very powerful gun.

Estimated age: twenty-eight.

Given the absence of any occupational deformities, it was likely that the man had never been employed in regular manual work. On the other hand, he had practised sports, especially rowing and boxing.

In perfect health. Remarkably hale and hearty. A scar on the left shoulder indicated that the young man had been hit in the shoulder-blade around three years ago by a bullet from a revolver.

Some compression of the fingertips was evidence that the stranger must have done a lot of typing.

Maigret read slowly, puffing gently on his pipe,

sometimes pausing to watch the Seine flowing past in the blazing morning sunshine. At other times, he jotted down a couple of words intelligible only to him in his notebook, which was famous for its ordinariness and because, having been used for years, it was full of higgledy-piggledy annotations, one on top of the other, and it was a wonder that Maigret could make any sense of them.

The laboratory report was no more sensational. The items of clothing had been worn by others before belonging to their last owner and everything suggested that he had bought them at the clothes market at the Carreau du Temple or from a second-hand goods dealer.

Same origin for the cane and the button boots.

The wig, of quite good quality, was nondescript, a model that could be bought from any wig-maker.

Lastly, analysis of the dust found on the clothes revealed quite a large amount of ultra-fine flour, not pure flour, but flour still mixed with bran husks.

Pince-nez: with flat lenses, of no use for correcting eyesight.

From Records, nothing! No file with fingerprints matching those of the victim.

Maigret sat deep in thought for a while, his elbows on his desk, and perhaps he was overcome by a certain laziness? The case looked neither promising nor unpromising, but more unpromising however, since fate, usually quite kind, was not offering the slightest help.

Madame Maigret's Suitor

Eventually he stood up, put on his hat, and went up to the duty clerk in the corridor.

'If anyone asks for me, I'll be back in an hour or so.'

He was too close to Place des Vosges to take a taxi, so he went on foot, along the banks of the Seine. He spotted Madame Maigret in the greengrocer's on Rue des Tournelles, engaged in an animated conversation with three or four busybodies.

He looked away to hide his smile and kept walking.

When Maigret had been just starting out in the police, one of his superiors, who was obsessed with scientific methods, which were very new at the time, was in the habit of saying to him:

'Be careful, young man! Not so much imagination! Police work isn't based on hunches but on evidence!'

Which had not stopped Maigret from going on to carve out a rather successful career.

And so, now that he'd reached Place des Vosges, he was less concerned with the technical details contained in the reports of that morning than with what he would have readily called the 'atmosphere' of the murder.

He tried to picture the victim, no longer dead as he had seen him, but alive: that young man of twenty-eight, fairhaired, robust, well built, probably stylish, dressing each morning in the costume of an aged beau, that suit perhaps bought from the flea market, beneath which he still wore fine linen.

Walking around the square twice then heading off down Rue de Turenne.

Where was he going? What did he do until three

o'clock in the afternoon? Did he stay disguised as a hero out of a farce by Labiche or did he change somewhere nearby?

How was he then able to sit still for three hours on end, on a bench, without opening his mouth, not moving a muscle, staring into space?

How long had this game been going on?

And finally, at night, where did the stranger vanish to? What was his private life like? Who did he see? Who did he talk to? To whom did he reveal the secret of his inner self? Why the flour and bran husks on his clothing? That suggested a flour mill, not a bakery. What did he get up to in a flour mill?

Maigret forgot to stop in front of 17A and had to retrace his steps. He passed under the arches and spoke to the concierge. She didn't bat an eyelid when he showed her his police badge.

'What do you want?'

'I should like to know which of your residents employs an attractive, stylish, blonde maid—'

She broke in, already sure of herself:

'Mademoiselle Rita?'

'It could well be. Every afternoon, she takes two children for a walk in the gardens.'

'Her employers' children. That's Monsieur and Madame Krofta, who have lived on the first floor for more than fifteen years. They were even here before me. Monsieur Krofta has an import–export business. He probably has offices in Rue du 4-Septembre.'

'Is he at home?'

Madame Maigret's Suitor

'He's just gone out, but Madame must be up there.'

'What about Rita?'

'I don't know. I haven't seen her yet this morning. That said, I was doing my stairs.'

A few moments later, Maigret pressed the bell on the first floor and let it ring for a long time, because even though he could hear distant sounds coming from the apartment, it was a while before the door was opened. He rang again. At last, the front door opened a fraction. He glimpsed a youngish woman who was trying to conceal her body because she was scantily dressed in a pale-blue bathrobe.

'Can I help you?'

'I wish to speak to Monsieur or Madame Krofta. I am a detective inspector from the Police Judiciaire.'

She reluctantly opened the door, pulling her bathrobe tight around her, and Maigret entered a sumptuous apartment, with vast, high-ceilinged rooms, tastefully furnished and with valuable ornaments.

'I apologize for receiving you like this, but I am alone with the children. How come you are already here? My husband left barely a quarter of an hour ago.'

She was a foreigner as was evident from her slight accent and typical Eastern European charm. Maigret had already recognized her as the woman in the light-coloured suit he had noticed that morning listening to the gossips in the middle of Place des Vosges.

'Were you expecting me?' he muttered, trying to hide his surprise.

'You or another. But I have to say I didn't realize that

the police were so quick. I assume that my husband will be back?'

'I don't know.'

'Did you not see him?'

'No.'

'So why . . . ?'

There was plainly a misunderstanding and Maigret, who stood only to gain information from it, did nothing to clear it up.

The young woman, for her part, perhaps to give herself time to think, stuttered:

'Would you excuse me for a moment? The children are in the bathroom, and I wonder if they're up to some mischief.'

She sashayed out of the room; she was truly beautiful, both in body and face, and as well as gracefulness she had a certain majesty in her bearing.

She could be heard in the bathroom talking to the children in an undertone, and then she returned, giving a faint welcoming smile.

'I'm sorry, I didn't even invite you to sit down. I would have liked my husband to be here, because he knows the value of the jewels better than I do since he's the one who bought them.'

What jewels was she talking about? And what did this new element mean, and the slight anxiety of the young woman who was so impatient for her husband to come home?

She seemed afraid to speak, dragging out the conversation to avoid saying anything compromising.

Maigret, who sensed this, took care to help her and looked at her with as neutral an expression as possible, putting on what he called his 'jovial fatso face'.

'You're always reading about thefts in the newspapers, but strangely you never think it can happen to you.

'Last night, I didn't have the least suspicion. It was this morning—'

'When you came back?' prompted Maigret.

She gave a start.

'How do you know I went out?'

'Because I saw you.'

'Were you already in the area?'

'I am here all year round because I am one of your neighbours.'

This worried her. She was clearly wondering what was behind those words that were puzzling in their simplicity.

'I did indeed go out, as I often do, for some fresh air before getting the children washed and dressed. That's why you find me in my bathrobe. When I come home, I put on indoor wear and . . .'

She could not repress a sigh of relief. Footsteps had stopped on the landing. A key turned in the lock.

'My husband . . .' she murmured.

And she called out:

'Boris! Come in here. There's someone waiting to see you.'

Well, the man was also very distinguished-looking – older than her, mid-forties, elegant, well dressed, Hungarian or Czech, thought Maigret, but speaking perfect French, his words carefully chosen.

'The inspector arrived before you and I was telling him that you would be back soon.'

Boris Krofta studied Maigret with a polite attention that disguised his wariness to some extent.

'Forgive me,' he murmured, 'but I do not entirely understand . . .'

'Detective Chief Inspector Maigret, from the Police Judiciaire.'

'That is odd. And do you wish to speak to me?'

'To the employer of a certain Rita who used to take two children for a walk around Place des Vosges every afternoon.'

'Yes . . . But you are not going to tell me that you have found her already, or that you have recovered the jewellery? I know you must think me strange. What an odd coincidence. To think that I have only just come back from the local police station where I went to file a complaint against Rita. And then I get home to find you here and you tell me . . .'

There was a jitteriness about him. It did not occur to his wife to leave the two men alone and she stared at Maigret with curiosity.

'What was the nature of your complaint?'

'The theft of the jewellery. That girl vanished yesterday, without giving us notice. I thought she had run off with a lover and I promised myself to place an ad in the newspaper this morning. Last night, we didn't leave the house. This morning, while my wife was out, it suddenly occurred to me to look in her jewellery box. That was when I realized why Rita had run away, because the box was empty.'

'What time was it when you discovered the theft?'

'Barely nine a.m. I was in my bathrobe. As soon as I was dressed, I dashed to the police station.'

'At this juncture, your wife came back?'

'That is correct. While I was getting dressed. What I still don't understand is that you came here this morning.'

'Mere coincidence!' muttered Maigret in an easy-going tone.

'And yet, I'd like to be informed. Did you know this morning that the jewellery had been stolen?'

An evasive gesture from Maigret, which meant nothing and had the effect of heightening Boris's nervousness.

'At least will you do me the kindness of telling me the reason for your visit? I do not think that the French police are in the habit of going into private homes, sitting down and—'

'And listening to what people tell them!' Maigret finished off. 'You'll admit that it's not my fault. Since I've been here, you have spoken to me about a jewellery theft which is of no interest to me, whereas I came about a murder—'

'A murder?' exclaimed the young woman.

'Were you not aware that a murder was committed yesterday on Place des Vosges?'

He saw her visibly rack her brains, recall that Maigret had told her that he was her neighbour and, whereas she might have said no, she murmured with a smile:

'I vaguely heard about something, this morning, when I was walking across the gardens. Some gossips were gathered—'

'I do not see what—' broke in the husband.

'. . . What this case has to do with you? Nor do I, so far, but I am certain that we'll find out sooner or later. What time did Rita disappear yesterday afternoon?'

'Just after five o'clock,' replied Boris Krofta without a hint of hesitation. 'Isn't that so, Olga?'

'That's right. She returned at five with the children. She went up to her room and I didn't hear her come down. At around six o'clock, I went up, because I was surprised that she wasn't cooking dinner. But her room was empty.'

'Would you show it to me?'

'My husband will take you up. It's awkward for me in this bathrobe.'

Maigret already knew the layout because it was exactly the same as his own apartment. After the second floor, the staircase became narrower and gloomier still, and you eventually reached the attic rooms. Krofta opened the third one.

'This is it. I left the key in the lock.'

'Your wife just said that she was the one who came up!'

'That is correct. But afterwards, I also came up.'

The open door revealed a servant's room that would have been ordinary, with its iron bedstead, wardrobe and washbasin, were it not for the view of Place des Vosges from the skylight.

Next to the wardrobe was a fibre suitcase of the sort

Madame Maigret's Suitor

that was sold widely. Inside the wardrobe, clothing and linen.

'It appears that your maid left without taking her belongings?'

'I suppose she preferred to take the jewellery, which is worth around two hundred thousand francs.'

Maigret's chubby fingers fiddled with a little green hat, then picked up another, trimmed with a yellow ribbon.

'Could you tell me how many hats your maid had?'

'I don't know. My wife might be able to tell you, but I doubt it.'

'How long had she been working for you?'

'Six months.'

'Did you find her through an advertisement?'

'Through an employment agency, which gave her a glowing recommendation. Her work, by the way, was impeccable.'

'Do you have any other servants?'

'My wife insists on looking after the children herself, which explains why we only need one maid. What is more, we spend most of the year on the Côte d'Azur where we have a gardener and his wife who help us.'

Maigret felt the need to blow his nose, despite the season; then he dropped his handkerchief and picked it up.

'That's odd,' he grunted, straightening up.

Then, looking Boris Krofta up and down, he opened his mouth and shut it again.

'Did you want to say something?'

'I wanted to ask you another question. But it is so indiscreet that you will find it offensive.'

'Please go ahead!'

'You insist? Well, I wanted to ask you if by any chance, given that your maid was very pretty, you might have had relations with her other than those of employer and employee. A standard question, you see, and one which you do not need to feel obliged to answer.'

Curiously, Krofta paused to think, suddenly a lot more worried. He took his time, looking about him slowly, then finally he sighed:

'Will my reply have to be made official?'

'There is every likelihood that that will never become necessary.'

'In that case, I'd rather admit that I did in fact—'

'In the apartment downstairs?'

'No. It's difficult, because of the children.'

'Did you meet outside?'

'Never! I came up here from time to time, and—'

'I understand the rest!' said Maigret with a smile. 'And I am very pleased with your reply. I had noticed that there was a button missing from your jacket sleeve. I have just found that button on the floor, at the foot of the bed. It is obvious that for it to be ripped off you would have been engaged in quite strenuous activity and . . .'

He held out the button and Krofta snatched it with surprising alacrity.

'When was the last time this took place?' asked Maigret reticently, heading for the door.

Madame Maigret's Suitor

'Three or four days ago. Wait! Yes, four days.'

'And was Rita willing?'

'I think so.'

'Was she in love with you?'

'At least she led me to believe so.'

'Are you aware of any rivals?'

'Oh, inspector! There was no question of that, and if Rita had had a suitor, I would not have considered him as a rival. I adore my wife and children, and I don't know myself why I . . .'

As he went down the stairs, Maigret couldn't help sighing:

'You, my friend, haven't stopped lying for one moment, I'm pretty sure!'

He stopped at the concierge's lodge and sat down facing the woman, who was shelling peas.

'So, have you seen them? They're very upset about this jewellery theft.

'Were you in your lodge at five o'clock yesterday afternoon?'

'Course I was. My son was even sitting where you are now, doing his homework.'

'Did you see Rita and the children come in?'

'As I'm seeing you now!'

'And did you see her come back down again a few minutes later?'

'That's what Monsieur Krofta came and asked me earlier. I told him that I didn't see anything. He says that's not possible, that I must have left my lodge, or that I wasn't paying attention. After all, so many people come in and out! But I think I'd have noticed her because that wasn't her usual time.'

'Have you ever run into Monsieur Krofta on the third-floor stairs?'

'What would he be doing up there? Oh! I get it. Perhaps you think he might have gone up there to see his maid? It's obvious you don't know Mademoiselle Rita. Now they're saying she's a thief. Maybe! But as far as running around or allowing herself to be taken advantage of by an employer . . .'

Resigned, Maigret lit his pipe and left.

3

'So, Detective Inspector Madame Maigret?' he teased fondly, planting himself in front of the window where his shirt-sleeves made two bright patches in the sunlight.

'So, you're going to have to be content with grilled meat and an artichoke. And I bought it ready-cooked to save time. Listening to all that gossip . . .'

'What are people saying? Come on, tell me the results of your investigation.'

'First of all, Mademoiselle Rita was not a maid.'

'How do you know?'

'All the shopkeepers noticed that she didn't know how to count in centimes, which shows she's never done household shopping. When the butcher wanted to give her the usual servant's discount, she looked at him in surprise and, if she accepted it, I'm sure it was so as not to draw attention to herself.'

Madame Maigret's Suitor

'Right! So, a girl from a good family who's playing at being a maid at Monsieur Krofta's . . .'

'I think she's more likely to be a student. In the local shops, nearly all languages are spoken – Italian, Hungarian, Polish . . . Apparently, she always seemed to understand and when someone told a joke in front of her, she'd smile.'

'And are they saying anything about your beau?'

'People had noticed him, but not as much as me. Oh yes! There's something else. The Gastambides' maid, who often goes and sits in the gardens in the afternoons, says that Rita didn't know how to crochet and that her handiwork would never have been any use except as a dish rag.'

Maigret's beady eyes laughed at his wife's efforts to gather together all her memories and express them with order and method.

'And that's not all! Before her, the Kroftas had a girl from their country who they fired because she was pregnant.'

'By Krofta?'

'Oh no! He's too besotted with his wife. Apparently, he's so jealous that they have almost no visitors.'

And so, every second, all these snippets, these statements true or false, changed the characters' profiles and sometimes contributed additional information.

'Since you've done such a good job,' muttered Maigret lighting a fresh pipe, 'I'm going to give you a tip-off. The shot that killed our stranger in a wig and pince-nez was fired from Rita's garret, and that will not be difficult to prove during a reconstruction. I've checked the angle of fire, which perfectly fits the position of the body and the trajectory of the bullet.'

'Do you think she was the one who—'

'I have no idea . . . Keep trying! . . .'

And, sighing, he put his collar and tie back on; she helped him into his jacket. Half an hour later, he sank into his chair at the Police Judiciaire and mopped his face, because the weather was even hotter than the day before and there was a storm in the air.

An hour later, Maigret's three pipes were hot, the ashtray full and the blotting pad covered in a jumble of words and random phrases. As for Maigret, he yawned, visibly sleepy, staring with his round eyes at everything he had written during his trance.

Supposing that Krofta had caused Rita to disappear, the theft of the jewellery was a clever way of diverting suspicion away from him.

That was well and good, but it proved nothing, and the maid could well have run off with her employer's jewellery.

Krofta had been loath to admit that he was his servant's lover.

That could mean that it was true and that it was an embarrassment for him; it could also mean that it was not true, but that he had caught Maigret picking up the button or that he suspected Maigret's question was some kind of trap.

The button would have been lying there for four

days, whereas the floor appeared to have been freshly swept.

And why had Madame Krofta gone out for a walk so early that morning? Why had she been reluctant to admit that she had heard about the murder, whereas Maigret had seen her hanging around the gossips for some time?

Why had Krofta asked the concierge if she had seen Rita go out?

A personal investigation? Was it not rather because he knew that the police would ask the same question and that, by speaking of it first, he had the opportunity to influence the good woman?

Abruptly, Maigret stood up. This whole jumble of minute details and comments ultimately not only annoyed him, but created in him a dull anxiety, because it was impossible not to end up asking:

'Where is Rita?'

On the run, if she had killed and stolen. But if she hadn't either killed or stolen, then . . .

A moment later, he was in the chief's office and, putting on a surly air, he said:

'Could you wangle a blank search warrant for me?'

'Are you serious?' laughed the head of the Police Judiciaire, who knew Maigret's moods better than anyone. 'We'll see what we can do. But you must be careful, all right?'

As if by chance, while the chief was dealing with the search warrant, Maigret received a telephone call. It was his wife, sounding worried:

'I've just thought of something. I don't know if I should say it over the phone . . .'

'Say it anyway!'

'Supposing it wasn't the woman who fired—'

'I understand. Go on.'

'Supposing, for instance, it was her employer. Are you with me? I wonder whether she might not still be in the apartment, by any chance? Maybe already dead? Or maybe held captive?'

It was touching to see Madame Maigret energetically pursuing a lead for the first time in her life.

But what Maigret was not admitting was that, in short, she had arrived at more or less the same point as him.

'Is that all?' he teased, all the same.

'Are you making fun of me? Do you not think that . . . ?'

'In other words, if we searched 17A from the cellar to the attic . . .'

'Just think, if she was still alive . . .'

'We'll see! In the meantime, try and see to it that dinner is a little more substantial than lunch.'

He hung up and found in the chief's office the warrant he had requested.

'Doesn't this have all the hallmarks of an espionage case to you, Maigret?'

But Maigret, when challenged, hated compromising himself and he merely shrugged.

Then, already in the corridor, he turned back, saying:

'I'll tell you this evening.'

Madame Maigret's Suitor

Madame Lécuyer, the concierge at 17A, was doubtless a good woman, who was doing her very best to raise her children decently, but her shortcoming was that she panicked easily.

'You understand,' she said, 'with all these people questioning me since this morning, I don't know whether I'm coming or going.'

'Calm down, Madame Lécuyer,' said Maigret, sitting by the window, not far from the boy, who, as on the previous day, was doing his homework.

'I've never harmed anyone and—'

'You're not being accused of harming anyone. I am simply asking you to try and remember. How many residents do you have?'

'Twenty-two, because I have to tell you that the second- and third-floor apartments are small, one and two bedrooms, which makes a lot of people.'

'Were none of these residents friendly with the Kroftas?'

'What do you imagine? The Kroftas are wealthy, with their car and their driver.'

'Incidentally, do you know where they park their car?'

'Somewhere around Boulevard Henri-IV. The driver hardly ever comes here, because he eats outside.'

'Did he come yesterday afternoon?'

'I'm not sure. I think he did.'

'With the car?'

'No! The car wasn't parked yesterday, or this morning. It's true that the employers haven't been out to speak of.'

'I see! Was the driver in the building at around five o'clock yesterday?'

'No! He left at half past four. I remember because my boy had just come home from school.'

'That's right!' her son agreed, looking up.

'Now, another question: did any large parcels leave here after five o'clock yesterday? For example, did a removals lorry park nearby?'

'Definitely not!'

'No one took out any furniture, or packing cases or bulky parcels?'

'What do you want me to say?' she moaned. 'How am I supposed to know what you mean by a bulky parcel?'

'A parcel that might, for instance, contain a human body.'

'Jesus, Mary! Is that what you're thinking? Are you suggesting that someone has been killed in my building?'

'Let's go over your recollections, hour by hour.'

'No! I didn't see anything of the sort.'

'No lorry, no cart, not even a barrow, came into the courtyard?'

'No, I'm telling you!'

'Are there no empty rooms here? Are all the apartments occupied?'

'Every single one! There was only one unoccupied room, on the third floor, and it was rented out two months ago.'

Just then, the boy looked up and, with his penholder between his teeth, he said:

'What about the piano, Mama?'

'What's that got to do with it? It's not a package that was taken out, but a package that came in. They even had a real struggle to get it up the stairs!'

'A piano was delivered?'

'Yesterday, at half past six.'

'Which company?'

'I don't know. There was no name on the lorry. It didn't drive into the courtyard. There was a huge crate and three men worked for a good hour.'

'Did they take the crate away with them?'

'No. Monsieur Lucien came down with the delivery men to buy them a drink at the bar on the corner.'

'Who is this Monsieur Lucien?'

'The tenant in the small room I told you about. He's been up there for two months. He's very quiet, very proper. Apparently, he's a composer.'

'Does he know the Kroftas?'

'I bet he's never even seen them.'

'Was he at home yesterday at five o'clock?'

'He came in at around half past four, about when the driver was leaving.'

'Did he tell you he was having a piano delivered?'

'No. He simply asked if there was any mail for him.'

'Did he receive much?'

'Very little.'

'Thank you, Madame Lécuyer. Stay calm. There's no need to worry.'

Maigret left, gave instructions to two inspectors who were pacing up and down Place des Vosges, then he went back into the building, hastily passing the concierge's lodge to avoid her asking him more questions and telling him how worried she was.

Maigret did not stop on the first floor, or on the second. On the third, leaning over, he noticed the scratch marks the piano had made as it was hauled up the stairs by the men. The scuffs seemed to stop at the fourth door, and he knocked, heard muffled footsteps, like those of an old woman in slippers, then a cautious voice mumbling:

'Who is it?'

'Monsieur Lucien, please?'

'It's next door.'

But at the same time, another voice stammered a few words, and the door opened a little. A fat old woman tried to make out Maigret's face in the gloom.

'Monsieur Lucien's not here for now, but perhaps I could give him a message?'

Without thinking, Maigret leaned in to peep at the second person who was inside the room.

In the half-light, you could barely see. The room was cluttered with ancient furniture, old fabrics and hideous knick-knacks and it reeked of that smell that is peculiar to the homes of the elderly.

Near the sewing machine sat a woman, bolt upright like a person visiting, and Maigret was more astonished than he had ever been in his life on recognizing his own wife.

4

'I found out that Mademoiselle Augustine took in small sewing jobs,' said Madame Maigret hastily. 'I came to see

Madame Maigret's Suitor

her about an alteration. We had a chat. She has the room next to that of the maid who stole.'

Maigret shrugged, wondering what his wife was leading up to.

'The strangest thing is that yesterday a piano was delivered to the other neighbour, a huge crate, which must still be there.'

This time Maigret winced, furious that his wife had come to the same conclusions as him, goodness knows how.

'Since Monsieur Lucien isn't here, I'll have to go downstairs,' he said.

And he didn't waste a moment. He brought in the two inspectors he'd left on Place des Vosges in front of the building, and positioned them on the stairs, near the Kroftas' door. A locksmith was called, as well as the chief inspector of the local police station.

Shortly afterwards, the door to Monsieur Lucien's room was forced open. Inside the room was just an ordinary piano, a bed, a chair, a wardrobe and, against the wall, the crate in which the piano had been delivered.

'Open that crate,' ordered Maigret, who was taking a big gamble and was deeply afraid.

He didn't want to touch it himself, for fear of finding it empty. He pretended to fill his pipe, as he pretended not to jump when someone shouted:

'Inspector! A woman!'

'I know!'

'She's alive!'

And he repeated:

'I know!'

Of course! From the moment there was a woman in the crate, it had to be the notorious Rita and he was almost certain that she was alive, tightly bound and gagged!

'Try and bring her round. Call a doctor.'

He walked past his wife, who was in the corridor with Mademoiselle Augustine and who gave him a smile that was unique in the annals of their marriage, a smile that would have him believe that Madame Maigret was going to abandon her role of submissive wife and become a detective.

As Maigret reached the first floor, the door of the Kroftas' apartment opened. Krofta was there in person, agitated but self-controlled.

'Is Monsieur Maigret not here?' he asked the two inspectors standing guard.

'I'm here, Monsieur Krofta.'

'There's a phone call for you. From the Ministry of the Interior.'

That was not entirely true. It was the head of the Police Judiciaire who was telephoning his subordinate.

'Is that you, Maigret? . . . I was certain I'd be able to get hold of you there . . . While you were up to goodness-knows-what in the building, the fellow whose apartment I called to speak to you phoned his embassy . . . The embassy alerted Foreign Affairs . . . Foreign Affairs—'

'I understand!' grunted Maigret.

'I told you so! An espionage case! The word is to keep it hush-hush, avoid saying anything to the press. For a long time, Krofta has been the unofficial agent in France for his country; he's the one who coordinates all the secret agents' reports.'

Krofta stood in a corner of the room, pale but smiling.

'Can I offer you a drink, inspector?'

'No, thank you!'

'I hear you have found my maid?'

And Maigret replied, hammering out each syllable:

'I found her in time, yes. Goodbye, Monsieur Krofta!!'

'As for me,' said Madame Maigret, finishing her chocolate cream, 'when I was told that that girl didn't know how to crochet . . .'

'Of course!' agreed her husband.

'Did they really manage to communicate interesting things to each other through that system, for hours each day? In short, if I understand correctly, this girl, this Rita who entered into service with the Kroftas as a maid, in fact spent her time spying on her employers?'

Maigret never liked explaining a case, but this time it would have been too cruel to leave Madame Maigret in the dark.

'She was spying on spies!' he grunted.

And, gruffly, shrugging his shoulders:

'That is why, just when I can at last lay hands on the gang, I'm ordered:

"Back off! Silence and discretion!"'

'It's true that it's not very pleasant,' she sighed as if forgiving all of Maigret's past ill humour.

'Quite a case, all the same, interspersed with flashes of genius. You can understand the situation. The Kroftas, on the one hand, all the intelligence that passes through their hands, which they pass on to their government . . .

'On the other hand, a cleaning woman and a man, Rita and the old gentleman on the bench, your strange suitor. Who are they working for? Now, that's none of my business. It's the turn of the foreign military intelligence agency. Most likely they're agents for another power, perhaps also from an opposing faction, because the domestic and foreign policies of some countries are curiously intricate.

'The fact remains that they need the intelligence centralized each day by Krofta, and Rita gets hold of that intelligence without too much difficulty, but how to transmit it outside? Spies are wary. The slightest suspicious move would be her downfall.

'Hence the idea of the elderly beau and the bench! The idea too of crocheting, which, manipulated by hands more expert than they appear, was in fact transmitting strings of long messages in Morse code.

'Facing Rita, her accomplice memorized everything. It is one more example of the incredible patience of some secret agents, because he had to retain every word of what he had just learned, for hours on end, until in his lodgings in Corbeil, near Moulins, he would spend the night typing it up.

'I wonder how this clever game was discovered by the Kroftas. Probably through the driver who, at around four, brought the news?'

Madame Maigret listened without daring to display the slightest emotion, so afraid was she that Maigret would stop.

'Now, you know as much as I do. For the Kroftas, it was a matter of doing away with the man first, and then grilling Rita to find out from her who she worked for and what services she had already rendered.

'A long time ago, Krofta installed a henchman in his building, Monsieur Lucien, who is an ace marksman. He calls him. Monsieur Lucien arrives, doesn't waste a minute and, from the young woman's room, shoots the enemy pointed out to him with an air rifle.

'No one sees anything or hears anything, except Rita who must be bringing the children home and who must keep up a pretence for fear of being killed too.

'She knows what awaits her. They try to drag her secret out of her. She holds firm. They threaten to kill her and then have that piano delivered to Monsieur Lucien, the crate of which will serve to remove her body. Besides, who would go looking for her in the musician's room?

'Already Krofta is orchestrating his defence, lodges a complaint, announces the disappearance of his maid, invents the theft of his wife's jewellery and . . .'

Silence. Dusk was falling. The sky was turning dark blue, and the fountains' silvery music blended with the liquid silver moonlight.

'And you handled it!' burst out Madame Maigret with admiration.

He looked at her half in earnest, half in jest. She went on:

'It's infuriating that just as you solved it, you weren't allowed to see it through.'

Then he, in mock annoyance:

'Do you know what's even more infuriating? It's having found you at that Mademoiselle Augustine's! In other words, you were on the scene before me. Then again, it did involve your suitor!'

« Certes, ils préfèrent que je ne voie pas certaines choses. Mais ce qu'il ne faut surtout pas, c'est que je leur en raconte d'autres ».

« – Vous direz tout?
– Et vous?
– J'essaierai. Si je n'y parviens pas, je m'en voudrais toute ma vie »

Peuples qui ont faim, 1934

PENGUIN ARCHIVE

H. G. Wells *The Time Machine*
M. R. James *The Stalls of Barchester Cathedral*
Jane Austen *The History of England by a Partial, Prejudiced and Ignorant Historian*
Edgar Allan Poe *Hop-Frog*
Virginia Woolf *The New Dress*
Antoine de Saint-Exupéry *Night Flight*
Oscar Wilde *A Poet Can Survive Everything But a Misprint*
George Orwell *Can Socialists be Happy?*
Dorothy Parker *Horsie*
D. H. Lawrence *Odour of Chrysanthemums*
Homer *The Wrath of Achilles*
Emily Brontë *No Coward Soul Is Mine*
Romain Gary *Lady L.*
Charles Dickens *The Chimes*
Dante *Hell*
Georges Simenon *Stan the Killer*
F. Scott Fitzgerald *The Rich Boy*
Katherine Mansfield *A Dill Pickle*
Fyodor Dostoyevsky *The Dream of a Ridiculous Man*

Franz Kafka *A Hunger-Artist*
Leo Tolstoy *Family Happiness*
Karen Blixen *The Dreaming Child*
Federico García Lorca *Cicada!*
Vladimir Nabokov *Revenge*
Albert Camus *A Short Guide to Towns Without a Past*
Muriel Spark *The Driver's Seat*
Carson McCullers *Reflections in a Golden Eye*
Wu Cheng'en *Monkey King Makes Havoc in Heaven*
Friedrich Nietzsche *Ecce Homo*
Laurie Lee *A Moment of War*
Roald Dahl *Lamb to the Slaughter*
Frank O'Connor *The Genius*
James Baldwin *The Fire Next Time*
Hermann Hesse *Strange News from Another Planet*
Gertrude Stein *Paris France*
Seneca *Why I am a Stoic*
Snorri Sturluson *The Prose Edda*
Elizabeth Gaskell *Lois the Witch*
Sei Shōnagon *A Lady in Kyoto*
Yasunari Kawabata *Thousand Cranes*
Jack Kerouac *Tristessa*
Arthur Schnitzler *A Confirmed Bachelor*
Chester Himes *All God's Chillun Got Pride*

Bram Stoker *The Burial of the Rats*
Czesław Miłosz *Rescue*
Hans Christian Andersen *The Emperor's New Clothes*
Bohumil Hrabal *Closely Watched Trains*
Italo Calvino *Under the Jaguar Sun*
Stanislaw Lem *The Seventh Voyage*
Shirley Jackson *The Daemon Lover*
Stefan Zweig *Chess*
Kate Chopin *The Story of an Hour*
Allen Ginsberg *Sunflower Sutra*
Rabindranath Tagore *The Broken Nest*
Søren Kierkegaard *The Seducer's Diary*
Mary Shelley *Transformation*
Nikolai Leskov *Night Owls*
Willa Cather *A Lost Lady*
Emilia Pardo Bazán *The Lady Bandit*
W. B. Yeats *Sailing to Byzantium*
Margaret Cavendish *The Blazing World*
Lafcadio Hearn *Some Japanese Ghosts*
Sarah Orne Jewett *The Country of the Pointed Firs*
Vincent van Gogh *For Art and for Life*
Dylan Thomas *Do Not Go Gentle Into That Good Night*
Mikhail Bulgakov *A Dog's Heart*
Saadat Hasan Manto *The Price of Freedom*

Gérard de Nerval *October Nights*
Rumi *Where Everything is Music*
H. P. Lovecraft *The Shadow Out of Time*
Christina Rossetti *To Read and Dream*
Dambudzo Marechera *The House of Hunger*
Andy Warhol *Beauty*
Maurice Leblanc *The Escape of Arsène Lupin*
Eileen Chang *Jasmine Tea*
Irmgard Keun *After Midnight*
Walter Benjamin *Unpacking My Library*
Epictetus *Whatever is Rational is Tolerable*
Ota Pavel *How I Came to Know Fish*
César Aira *An Episode in the Life of a Landscape Painter*
Hafez *I am a Bird from Paradise*
Clarice Lispector *The Burned Sinner and the Harmonious Angels*
Maryse Condé *Tales from the Heart*
Audre Lorde *Coal*
Mary Gaitskill *Secretary*
Tove Ditlevsen *The Umbrella*
June Jordan *Passion*
Antonio Tabucchi *Requiem*
Alexander Lernet-Holenia *Baron Bagge*
Wang Xiaobo *The Maverick Pig*